PETTY BETTY

Revenge is a Dish Best Served with Glitter

PETTY BETTY REVENGE SERVICES
BOOK 1

RUBY SMOKE

BLURB

Dating is a cluster fu*<. Relationships? A fu*< of clusters.
But worst of all are the assholes that get away with it.
Not anymore...

Have you ever dreamed of getting revenge on someone who wronged you?

Betsey and her friends have. During their weekly girls' night, fueled by too many shots and too much gossip, they create Petty Betty - a mastermind of revenge who will stop at nothing to make things right.

Glitter in vents, missing chargers, and boxes of dildos delivered to the wrong place - there are no limits to how far Petty Betty and her friends will go to get even.

But when Betsey's first target turns out to be the man of her dreams, things get complicated. Nathan is everything she's ever wanted, but she can't let go of her desire for revenge.

As Betsey and Nathan's relationship grows, the line between revenge and romance becomes blurred.
Can she have it all - love and revenge - or will she have to choose?

In this hilarious romantic comedy, readers will be swept into a tale of full of lovable, relatable characters and unexpected twists and turns while they navigate redemption, and the power of friendship.

Join Betsey and her friends on a journey of self-discovery and hilarious mishaps that's sure to keep you laughing until the very end.

'Petty Betty' will have you rooting for true love to win.
Ruby Smoke is serving you revenge on a platter in this Romantic Comedy.
Get ready for a wild ride of love, laughter, and a lotta bit of payback in this hilarious novel.

COPYRIGHT

COPYRIGHT

Petty Betty

Ruby Smoke

First published in Great Britain in [2023] by **DIRTY TALK PUBLISHING LIMITED**

First published Great Britain in [2023] by [Ruby Smoke & Isabella Phoenix]

This edition published in [2023] by **DIRTY TALK PUBLISHING LIMITED**

Copyright © [2023] by [**Ruby Smoke**]

The moral right of [Ruby Smoke] to be identified as the author of this work has been asserted by him in accordance with the Copyright, Designs and Patents Act 1988.

All the characters in this book are fictitious, and any resemblance to actual persons living or dead, is purely coincidental.

All rights reserved. No part of this publication may be reproduced in any form or by any electronic or mechanical means, including information storage and retrieval systems, or transmitted in any form or by any means without the prior permission in writing of the copyright owner, except for the use of quotation in book reviews.

To request permission, contact [**rubysmokeauthor@gmail.com**].

Edited by: **Ruby Smoke**

Cover Design: Alt 16 Designs

Published by **DIRTY TALK PUBLISHING LTD**

DEDICATION

To all the hopeless romantics, scorned exes, and adventurous daters, this one is for you!

May it bring laughter to your heart, revenge to your soul, and love to your life.

But most importantly, may it remind you never to settle for anything less than a good laugh, a great comeback, and a happily ever after.

But mainly a really good comeback with extra revenge sprinkled...
 -Ruby

AUTHOR NOTE

As you read Petty Betty, you will have the distinct pleasure of meeting our very feisty Kati Lopez, a young Latina who is very colorful with her language. She is pretty much the written character version of our own Ruby Smoke and her family full of *very spicy,* independent women. Any stereotypes depicted that may cause offense is unintentional, as these are all experiences of Ruby and her upbringing in Washington Heights, NYC, and the Bronx, NYC. Ruby's parents, grandparents, aunts, uncles, hell, and even her older sister, never spoke a lick of English until after a few years in the United States. Still, her mom was the manager of an Optical in Washington Heights where the population was mainly Latino, and everyone spoke Spanish. In fact, it was considered the "Little Dominican Republic." Eventually Ruby moved to The South Bronx where the population was mainly Puerto Rican. Her best friends and her husband were also children of immigrants! New York City is a cultural melting pot, and it led to a good understanding of mixed cultures, and it was certainly a wild ride!

Ruby grew up in what one would consider "the ghetto," as locals often called it. The truth is, she grew up in poor neighborhoods, strife with poverty and crime, but was blessed with a community of hard-working individuals who did everything to provide for their families. They did what they had to, to survive and the result? For her parents, four women who were accepted to top universities and moved on to provide more for their own families. For her aunts and uncles, all their children also ended up in great universities with wonderful careers.

This is said to show that despite everything, these backgrounds provide a certain passion and fortitude, both mental and physical. It also proves that difficult circumstances do not always result in sad endings, sometimes they are steppingstones to great ones! This is what you will see when you encounter Kati. Eventually, she will have her own book and she will dazzle you!

LATIN TERMS, PHRASES, INSULTS

*Keep in mind, some translations don't necessarily translate well into English, but language is complex. Especially when considering both regional and cultural slang! Also, we don't suggest running around cursing in Spanish (ha-ha) *

Maldito- Fucker

Coño- Fuck

Es Como Agua - It's like water!

Puto- Man Whore, but it is also the equivalent of both 'asshole' and 'fucking' depending on context.

'Qué cabrón'- means, literally, 'what a big male goat.' But it's used in the way we would say, 'what a bastard!' This curse is rarely used as an angry insult

La Concha De Tu Madre- Motherfucker, definitely not something to use in easy banter. Simply put... these are fighting words. LOL

Joder- this can also mean fuck, but it can also mean 'to bother' for example, you can say "El si jode." Which means, loosely, he really bothers.

No me joda- Feminine version of, don't bother me or

depending on context (like anger) it can mean don't fuck with me. The masculine *version would be jod(e)*

Mierda- Shit, or crap

Chapiodora- This is a Dominican slang word, that translates as 'gold-digger' and is only used in the Dominican Republic and a small number of islands in the Caribbean.

Pendejo/a — This is one of the most common Spanish insults, and it generally means "dumbass" (though it literally translates to "pubic hair").

Calmate- Calm down
Pero Sobre El Amor- But about love
Hombres- Men
Mujer- woman
No sé nada- I don't know anything
Amiga(o)- friend
Querida(o)- Loved one

REVENGE IS A DISH BEST SERVED WITH GLITTER

Chapter One

...BEST SERVED...

Betsey

"I mean, it's *horrible*." Lia flings herself dramatically into a chair with a loud groan, her blonde hair whipping around her face. "Why is dating so damn hard? And these apps?" she thrusts her phone in my face. "Fucking useless. I've gotten three dick pics and a marriage proposal this week alone. I mean, who *proposes* on an app?" She smacks her head onto the table with a loud thud.

I chuckle at her dramatics and place another cupcake in front of her slumped form. Then, like a shark, she lifts her head and darts her hand out before it can disappear and bites down with a moan.

"Like, why can't all dicks be as good as your cupcakes, Betsey?" she mumbles around the half-chewed cake.

"Ewww, Lia." Maeve sniffs at her, reaching for her fourth glass of wine. "At least finish your half-masticated food before you spray us all with your spit." Her cheeks quickly matched the tumbling red hair that flowed down her back like a fiery waterfall.

"Forget the cupcake spit; how about not getting hair in my

cake?" Kati demands, her Spanish accent more pronounced as she guzzles directly from her bottle of wine.

Lia runs a hand through her blonde hair, grimacing at the frosting, clumping some of her strands together.

My best friends continue to compare dating app stories while I slouch back against the plush booth of the bakery, sipping my drink. Every week without fail, on Sundays, we meet at my bakery, 'You Knead Sweets,' to bitch and moan about our love lives—or lack thereof, while getting ridiculously drunk. Sort of... a drunken purge before the new week starts. It wasn't the healthiest coping mechanism, but it was ours.

"I get so turned off by the entire dating scene. You know, this week alone, some guy came in with three different women to buy them one of my cupcake bouquets. *Three*," I shake my head, remembering the look on the women's faces, thinking they were the most special person in the world when they were just on one long sexual conveyor belt.

"Oh, yes. I know who you mean. Tall, dark, and Armani?" Kati sighs wistfully. "Why is it always the handsome ones that are assholes? *Pendejos.*" She knocks her bottle back again and takes a healthy swig.

"Yeah, stupid *Pendejos!*" Lia echoes her and lifts her glass in a salute.

I burst out laughing at the fire in Lia's tone. "You know that means the same thing, and now that Kati is switching over to Spanish, maybe we need to take the alcohol away." I jokingly reach for her bottle.

"Don't you fucking dare *Puta de azucar!*" she growls, cradling her bottle like a baby.

Maeve cackles, her glazed eyes sparkling with joy. "Sugar whore! That's a new one."

"I get called every type of whore when she wakes up in the morning. This morning I was a *Puta de zanahorias* because today's special was carrot cupcakes. She loves me; I feel it." I deadpan. They know that's Kati's love language.

And sure enough, she tuts. "If I didn't love you, I wouldn't insult you. It's a Latina rule. Besides, who the fuck makes five *hundred* cupcakes at four in the morning?" she groans, scrunching her nose up.

"*We* do, Kati. Bakery here," I gesture at myself and roll my eyes.

"Fuck. She's right. Why is she always right?" she glares at Maeve and Lia.

"It's a curse," Maeve replies solemnly.

"Okay. Back to the issue at hand. Guys like that serial bakery dater are the reasons we need to figure something out here." Her eyes shine with something that makes her look feral, and she hovers from her seat. "Women get the short end of the dick. We need some payback!" Lia ends her passionate tirade with her fists slamming onto the table, which nearly knocks Kati's bottle over, and she grabs it, shooting her a death glare.

Maeve shakes her head, ignoring our feral friend. "And what about our poor Betsey? She finally goes on a date with that guy Larry, and after two pumps, he's done!"

"I mean, with a name like Larry, that honestly should have been expected," Kati adds. We all nod in agreement.

The thought makes me cringe as I recall my date with him this past Monday. I thought it would go well. After all, Larry would come in daily, buy a cookie, and ask me for a date. I finally said yes after a month. Hell, a girl can only have a dry spell for so long before the vagina shrinks and disappears into a sexless vortex of darkness. No, it's true. Google said so.

The date started pleasantly enough. He was attentive, and the meal was delicious. After some flirting, I went back to his place, where everything went south. It probably would be an insult to call it sex after he literally went ten seconds and passed out right after. I am talking; full-blown snoring passed out. You would think the guy had performed at the sexual Olympics. Then, when I hastily threw my clothes on, with the worst case of lady blue balls, I saw a picture in a frame of him and a pretty blonde, with 'happy third anniversary' written in glittery cursive. Needless to say, I hightailed it out of there, and I've been ignoring his increasingly desperate messages since then.

"Super done with Larry. And he was in a relationship on top of that," I scowl, refilling my glass in annoyance.

"Exactly! Look at him wasting your vaginal juices. I'd bet you had more fun with your electric boyfriend after that, anyway." She shrugs and then leans forward. "So why not get revenge? Let's bring back 'Petty Betty'" Lia leans back with her drink raised, a satisfied smile on her face.

I snort with laughter—vaginal *juices*.

"Petty Betty?" Maeve asks, her eyes darting between Lia and me.

Kati gives a throaty chuckle. "In graduate school, Betsey got so drunk after a bad breakup that she started a website to expose cheating assholes. In two days, the website was the most talked about thing on campus. People would post proof of cheating and expose their boyfriends and exes. It was fucking priceless."

"Yeah. That was until Betsey took it down when someone posted a video of a professor fucking a freshman, and the campus went on a witch hunt trying to find the site's owner," Lia adds, rolling her eyes.

"Fucking, genius. This is a great idea. Lets' do it!" Maeve shouts, and I wince as it echoes around the empty bakery.

I need to be the sensible one here, even though I'm drunk. "We are missing the obvious problem here," I frown. It went without saying that even with staff, I was still waking up at 4 am and going to bed late, considering that after the store closed at 5, we stayed to clean and prep. I had no time to run a revenge website.

The others all make noises of disagreement. "I don't see a problem," Lia holds her fingers up. "Kati is a genius with advertising, marketing, and website development. Once we set it up, people can post. It will practically run itself." She shrugs like it's a done deal, Kati nodding in excitement next to her.

"That is so boring, however. Why not add a little extra... service... for a price, of course." Maeve grins mischievously.

That look from her didn't bode well for me. I really should get up and call it a night. Walk away. I open my mouth to say that, but my eyes widen as something else emerges. "What do you have in mind?"

That is how three hours, thirty cupcakes, and five bottles of alcohol later, 'The Petty Betty Revenge Service' was born. The only difference this time is that instead of the 'expose your ex' pages, we add a 'request a revenge' option. That's right. We would exact revenge on your cheating partner or ex for a fee. Despite her angry grumbles, I drew the line at Maeve's request to use the Irish mafia. Instead, we are settling on harmless but pain-in-the-ass pranks. What can I say? Revenge is a dish best served with a well-placed glitter bomb and monthly dildo delivery services.

Chapter Two
...SUIT UP, BITCHES...

Betsey

"Ugh. It feels like someone hit me with a truck, backed it up, then jumped out and beat me with a crowbar before doing it again." My voice is raspy as I pop the next set of cookies in the oven, taking the other batch out. I never thought that the scent of casting sugar and baked goods would make me feel sick, but I guess I am genuinely that hungover.

"*Ay Dios,* today is the day I die. I feel it." Kati mutters as she hunches over the dough she's kneading for an apple pie crust.

We usually get to the bakery by four thirty to start prep and baking. Except in this case, we never actually left. So by the time we completed the finishing touches on the Petty Betty website and toasted to the death of all dating apps with our ground-breaking app, it was already 3 am. Someone should have told us that toasting typically involves glasses instead of entire bottles of champagne, but here we are... dead. Maeve and Lia didn't even make it home; they were slumped in my office, drooling all over my desk. Lucky bitches.

"We should wake those two slackers to help us make all this

shit. *Putas*," she grumbles, and I huff out a laugh, then immediately regret it as my head protests the sound of any joy.

I am fortunate enough to have full-time staff that also come in to help in the day, but they usually work with headphones in, having already developed a smooth rhythm between themselves. So I leave the smaller, more basic desserts for them to prep, while I the more intricate ones that require a light hand, like my tiramisus or decorated cakes, I'm the one that manages it. Although, in my delicate state, I wasn't sure my hands were as light as I needed them to be.

"Fuck it, they will taste like mouth porn," I mutter aloud in answer to my brain as I continue piping.

"Amen, Sista." Kati fist pumps the air. "Also, my hangover remedy is ready, so chug it and buck the fuck up because we open in fifteen minutes."

She hands me a thick beige liquid, and I plug my nose with my fingers as I choke it down. It was like drinking my vomit, but credit to her, it was effective and helped us survive many Sunday night bitch sessions.

I glance at the large wall clock and take a deep breath. *Only 8 hours left. I can do this.*

Betsey

Thankfully, closing time comes around faster than expected, and soon we are locking the doors, my staff already out the back cleaning the kitchen and prepping for tomorrow. When I checked if they were okay, they waved me away. I was grateful to them for being able to handle it in there without me micromanaging them. Maeve and Lia rose from the dead a couple of hours after we opened and headed home to shower and change. They came back within an hour since I told them they were obligated to help. After all, it took four of us to tango, and mathematically speaking; they were as equally responsible for my hangover as I was.

I also may have skewed the friend math in my favor because I needed the help. Oh, well. The bakery was already famous, but throwing Maeve behind the counter was a recipe for madness. It wasn't just that she was gorgeous; she was, no, it was because Maeve was Texas's sweetheart. In the modeling world, her name is bigger than Naomi Campbell or Gisele Buchanan. Never mind, she was a rabid, red hair, sour patch queen to us. Her smile could even fool the pope.

I was grateful for her today, in any case. It meant we sold out damn quick, and we could lock up a couple of hours early.

My breath leaves me in a long sigh as I slump into my comfortable chair behind my small oak desk. I close my eyes for about two seconds before Lia comes running in with a high-pitched squeal, Maeve and Kati hot on her heels. My eyebrows twinge at the noise, and I glare at her. She is damn lucky Kati's hangover remedy was magical holy water, and the demonic headache was almost wholly exorcised from my body, or I would have stabbed her.

"Don't give me that look. We have our first customer for Petty Betty!" Lia claps, handing me her laptop.

My eyebrows go from furrowed to in my hairline while I read the message. "This person is paying us ten *thousand* dollars to get back at her boyfriend. For ghosting her? What? I didn't even know we charged that damn much!"

Lia shrugs and checks her nails out in a coy gesture. "We don't. But she was able to pay more."

Our eyes turn in unison to Kati, who designed the elaborate website and payment portal and set up paid advertisements in less than two hours. She's a tech genius under all that feistiness and *cafecitos*.

She throws her hands in the air. "Listen, you can't blame me for adding an extra charge for making an immediate booking. It says right there," she comes around to point at the tiny fine print at the bottom of the webpage. "If you need immediate revenge, there will be a surcharge. I think it was a fair fee."

"Genius," Lia slaps Kati's hand with a laugh.

Maeve nods in agreement, "It's true. We all have busy schedules, and sometimes I'm not even in the country. Immediate revenge should cost more. But how immediate is immediate?"

I shake my head, still taken aback that anyone would pay so much extra to get revenge. I mean, I knew there were plenty of scorned women out there, but nearly ten thousand dollars' worth of scorn? That's *a lot* of hostility.

I re-read the message that was sent before answering Maeve.

Boyfriend ghstd me. revge, tngt whle @ gym. Cr alwyz unlocqed. KareFitness, dwntown Dallas. Blck Maserati. lnc plte- InvstThs

"It's for tonight? Jesus, this message is barely understandable. She must have been drunk as fuck writing this," I mutter, shaking my head. She could spell Maserati, though. Figures.

"To be fair, we were drunk when we created the website—also, no takebacks. The refund clause is airtight. So, suit-up bitches! Time to get some fucking revenge!" Lia pulls a back out from behind her back, like fucking Houdini, and starts passing us black catsuits.

"When the fuck did you even have time to get this?" Maeve stared at the catsuit.

"Forget that; why the fuck do the outfits have the crotch cut out and rips down the sides?" Kati grimaces.

Lia shrugs as she strips off her clothes. "My assistant said it was all the store he went to had left. It's one size fits all."

I frown as I look at the tag, "yeah, I am sure 'BDSM Ecstasy'...." I roll my eyes, "had exactly *four* 'one-size-fits-all' porn suits. Your assistant is clearly a pervert."

"Here," she reaches back in the bag to pass us black panties.

"Put these panties on so your crotch matches. See?" she turns around and bends over. I admit the panties stopped the potential vaginal peepshow. She jumps up, grinning wildly.

"Can't believe I'm wearing this," I shake my head as I strip and pull on the tight suit.

"You? I look like one of those TikTok models!" Kati looks down at her outfit, her jaw unhinged.

I whistle. I mean, she's not wrong. Kati is damned hot, and the suit emphasizes her ridiculously curvaceous body. Add that to her lengthy hair, hazel eyes, and sexy accent; she was a wet dream.

Lia catcalls, "Well damn, Kati. The perfect revenge would be to offer that sweet ass on a platter and then snatch it away."

We giggle, taking in our highly inappropriate, stealthy 'revenge' gear. Then, after sweeping our hair back and putting on the black ballet flats Lia also had in her magical Mary Poppins bag, we were ready to go. Operation Petty Betty was a go.

Chapter Three
...CUPCAKE BANDIT STRIKES AGAIN...

Betsey

Our car sneaks into the gym parking lot right at the back in the shadows near the exit, so we can make a quick getaway once our mission is complete. But, of course, that tactic was all Kati's idea. I would ask how she knew that was the best course of action, except it was damned smart, so I didn't.

"Anyone see the Maserati we need to target?" Maeve whispers.

"It's right in the front." Lia whispers back.

Kati gives a low whistle. "Holy shit, that's a 2014 Maserati Alfieri Concept. Damn, it would be a crime to hurt that car."

"How the hell do you know that?" Lia whispers again with a frown.

I snap my fingers in their faces. "Why the fuck are we whispering?"

"Oh." Maeve's throat clears and then returns to normal. "I just figured it was best to stay in character," she shrugs, with a grin curling at her lip.

Kati raps her knuckles on the dash. "Uh, I just realized

something. What the fuck is the plan? How are we going to exact this revenge?"

Of course, we all turn to Lia, the mastermind of this entire operation, with expectant anticipation.

When her cheeks bloom with a rosy pink before looking away, we all groan in unison. She doesn't have a clue.

"You had enough time to get porn 'get away' outfits but didn't think to get the stuff we would need to actually *do* anything?" I shout at her in exasperation.

"Well, technically," Maeve interjects. "Lia had enough time to delegate her assistant to get the porn suits."

Lia glares at Maeve and then throws her hands in the air, a picture of innocence. "Well, I was invested in ensuring we got the outfits."

Maeve chips in. "Well, what is the plan? Ten-thousand dollars to what? Key up a beautiful car? I am *not* going down for property damage. I have a shoot in Maui next week. Nope. Sorry."

I had to agree with her on that one. Our entire revenge mission is supposed to be petty, not cause thousands of dollars worth of physical damage. Kati's forehead is creased with a frown, and she rubs at her bottom lip. Her tell, and if *she* looked conflicted about this situation, it probably wasn't the best of ideas. She was feisty, but underneath it all, she was one of the most practical of us.

Suddenly Lia throws the car door open and sprints around the back towards the trunk. Moments later, she jumps back into the front seat, a big brown bag clutched in her lap, her face bright. "I have the best idea! Last week, I had my assistant pick up a few things for an open house. He came back with two pounds of red glitter!" She shakes the bag.

We're silent for a beat before Maeve says what we're all thinking. "Jesus, your assistant is beyond fucking useless," she shakes her head. I mean, who the fuck *would* use two pounds of glitter? A PTA president?

Kati clicks her fingers. "I saw something like this on TikTok. Glitter bombs." She smirks. "Yeah. We can pour the glitter all over the car and in the air vents, so when he turns on the car...boom! It blasts him in the face."

Fucking genius. I narrow my eyes at the offending Maserati, already angry with the owner and so prepared to ruin his night. And most of his week. Maybe even the month. Glitter was not easy to get rid of, and in a car vent? He is going to be so fucked. *That will teach him to ghost his girlfriend. Pendejo.* I can't help but adopt my inner Kati.

With this new plan— or should I say the only one— the excitement is tangible as we all scramble out of the car and do a weird combination of a shuffle and some bizarre crouched spider run to the car. Strangely enough, despite being seven in the evening, only a few cars are dotted around the parking lot. Of course, it makes it a lot harder to hide, but we're creative. Plus, the amount we are being paid means being fully invested.

"Oh wait," Lia hisses at us, reaching into the bag strapped on her back. "Throw on these masks; this gym has cameras!" She chucks us masks one by one, which we hastily put on without looking correctly.

My eyebrows furrow at the sight of my best friends. "What the fuck? Why is your mask Wreck-It Ralph, Maeve's a Daffy Duck, and Kati's over there as Mrs. Incredible? What the fuck am I?" I hiss. They may have covered our faces, but these masks weren't inconspicuous. On the contrary, they were downright bright, entirely at odds with the black porn suits we had which helped us blend into the night.

"It was all my assistant could find," Wreck-It Ralph, aka Lia, says, laughter in her voice.

Maeve giggles. "You're perfect. One giant cupcake face."

The others dissolve into sniggers at my mask when they look just as silly. I throw my hands up in the air, "un-fucking believable. Come on. Let's get this done before someone notices cartoons and cakes running around in BDSM outfits. It's bad enough that my boobs are about to pop out the sides of this ridiculous getup."

We inch closer to the Maserati and cast our eyes about for anyone in the area, but it's just us. Lia opens the door, and Kati slinks around to open the other side, and then we go to town throwing glitter all over the seats, upholstery, cup holders, and trunk of the car. Once we have a sparkling interior, we carefully pour the excess into the vents.

"This guy is either stupid rich or cocky as hell to leave his car unlocked like this. Even in this posh ass gym," Maeve mutters and pauses. "Do you think this guy is some mafia bigshot? Doesn't matter if he is; I'll have my family destroy him." She cracks her knuckles and punches her fist, making a giggle tumble out of me. At this point, I am fully convinced she really does have Irish mafia ties.

"I doubt it; this car can't be hot-wired. It also has a state-of-the-art GPS monitoring system. If this was even moved, it would be found in minutes," Kati points at the blinking light on the sports car.

"Again, how the fuck do you even know this?" Lia grunts, leaning over to get some last-minute glitter under the car mats.

Kati shrugs nonchalantly, "I like cars. Doesn't hurt that I've also hot-wired a few just for shits and giggles. Wanted to know if the videos on YouTube were accurate. Call it science. But this would be a wet dream if you could even get to the wiring compartment. This baby is like Fort Knox."

We all stop to stare at her, just casually dropping that bombshell. I'm the first to break the silence. "You've hot-wired cars? Fuck, that's hot. Please marry me?"

"You're missing the point. She did it to study cars. Figures." Lia raises her eyebrows at our crazy friend. "Oh, look, a briefcase!" She's distracted by the discovery. "Let's put some in there!" She goes to open it but then curses. "Fuck, it's locked with alpha-numeric code."

Kati scoffs, "Give it to me. I'll open that bitch." She gets to work, and we poke our heads out to look around again. Our luck holds; no one is leaving the gym yet. Still, I nudge Kati to hurry up.

"Done! Pour that glitter bitches," she exclaims, holding the case out to Maeve, who's holding some in the palm of her hand. Kati could do anything if she puts her mind to it; she's fantastic.

Maeve quickly pours in the rest of the glitter and closes the briefcase as a voice behind us screams, "Hey!"

"Oh, shit! Time to go." I squeal as four men come running full pelt toward us. I curse myself not for not looking back to check for the gym doors opening again, having been so consumed by Kati picking the lock. We all scramble towards our car, helplessly laughing as we sprint towards our car in the ridiculous suit and masks, high on the adrenaline of finishing our first job. We finally get into the car and close the door, peeling off with a loud squeal. Lia slows down just enough to roll down the window and snap a photo for proof while she screams, "you've been Petty Bettied Bitch!!!"

"Fast and the Furious, *Pendejo!*"

"Payback is a bitch!" Maeve adds.

Feeling left out, I add, "The cupcake bandit strikes again!"

Then, we leave the scene of the crime and the four men scratching their heads.

Chapter Four
...THE INSIDE OF A STRIPPER'S PANTIES...

Nathan

"What the fuck!" I'm stunned into a frozen shock, taking in the state of my car.

Lawrence, the shit, is currently doubled over, laughing his ass off. "She said...she said..." he wheezes, "Cupcake...bandit." Tears streak down his face at the sight of my poor, poor Maserati.

Oskar prowls past me and around the car to open the door, chuckling when a cloud of red glitter flies out, then slowly falls to the floor. "Damn, who the hell did you piss off, man?"

A wave of dizziness hits me, and I force in a shaky breath and squeeze my eyes shut against the offensive sight. *Maybe when I open my eyes, my car will be back to normal.*

I groan as I open my eyes. It's all still there in horrifying technicolor. "Fuck. This cannot be happening."

Lawrence finally straightens out, wiping his eyes. "Your precious Maserati looks like the inside of a stripper's panties." Then, when a cloud of glitter flies up on a breeze, he loses it again and sinks to the floor, howling.

"I would say, more like the inside of a PTA president's home office," Oskar adds, swiping some of it onto his hands.

I glare at him, "not fucking helpful."

"Would it be helpful to add that whoever they are could wear the fuck out of those catsuits? If we ever catch them, I call dibs on the curvy model; she was fucking hot," Lawrence says wistfully. "My TikTok dream come to life."

The usually silent Ivor chimes in. "She had a Mrs. Incredible mask on." He watches as Oskar picks some more glitter into his hands and then blows it away like he's fucking Tinkerbell.

"Yeah, dude. She had that mask on for her incredible curves," Lawrence scoffs, pushing himself off the floor.

Oskar gives an infuriating smirk. "I call dibs on Wreck-It-Ralph, anyone who can pull off a Ralph mask and a catsuit, is my kind of woman."

Little Miss Cupcake's breasts nearly popping out of that ridiculous catsuit to say hello was almost enough to make me forget my current situation. *Almost*.

I shake my head. "Can we focus? What the fuck am I supposed to do about my car?" I bellow. They, of course, continued talking as if I didn't even speak.

"I don't know. That tall one is right up my alley. I wouldn't have to hurt my back to reach her," Ivor chuckles. We stare at him; he doesn't laugh often. In fact, I could count on one hand the times the stoic man has laughed in our presence.

His face goes blank under the weight of our stares, and he shrugs, "what? she had a Daffy Duck mask. I'm a sucker for Looney Tunes."

"I don't even have the energy to dissect that. Any of you want to try?" Lawrence asks, meeting my gaze and Oskar's. We shake our heads, and Ivor rolls his eyes.

I sigh, scrubbing a hand over my hair. "Fuck you guys; I am going home and calling a detailer to come out and fix this mess," I stomp over to the car door and try, and fail, to get the glitter off the seat. Finally, with a growl, I sit down, and a cloud of glitter poofs up around me like a mini glitter storm. I scowl as the three of them stand outside, Ivor looking on in amusement while Oskar and Lawrence hold each other up. Sticking up a glittery middle finger, I turn the car on and immediately regret my life choices as a plume of red glitter comes flying out of the vent. I yell, and cough as the shit gets into my mouth, coating my hair and entire body. *Oh, whoever the fuck did this was going to pay.*

"Fuck, you guys!" I yell out the window as I tear out of the parking lot, leaving my so-called friends dying of laughter at my misfortune, and drive home, looking like an art project gone very, very wrong.

Chapter Five

...FUCKING, CUPID...

Nathan

"Yes, Dad, I will go to the bakery to place the order in person...no, I won't have one of the assistants do it...no Lawrence won't do it either...yes, I know last time he ordered dick-shaped cakes." I roll my eyes at my friend as my dad talks my ear off about the importance of ordering this myself, even as I am walking to the bakery to order my mom some fancy cupcake bouquet for her birthday next week.

"Hey! I'll have you know those Bavarian cream dicks were the chef's kiss. Or I kissed the chef. Doesn't matter. They were delicious!" Lawrence exclaims loudly, drawing the bemused gazes of people passing by in the streets. Some guy even screams back at him. "Right on, you lick that cream, brother," fist pumping. I grin at their antics while Oskar laughs, and Ivor shakes his head without so much as a lip twitch.

"See? *That* guy knows all about them. Fucking tasty ass dicks," he mutters, and I stare at him with my brows raised, incredulous. *Why the fuck am I friends with this guy?*

I turn my attention back to dad, who is still talking. "No, the others are just coming with me. I'm going to be the one making the order. You know Tuesdays are our weekly lunch meetings. *No*, they are not *man-dates...* Why *shouldn't* I call it that? Well, gee, maybe because calling it a man date is weird; dad...fine. I'll settle for bachelor meetings." A grin stretches across my lips as his loud laugh bellows through the phone and promptly ends the call on me. My father is one of a kind. It takes a particular person to build a cutthroat Investment Firm from the ground up in one of the best-known business cities in country. My mother also worked at the firm, and I'm not sure how they managed it all, but they always made each other and me feel special. Loved. He says that the day he met my mother, he felt a passion ignite that opened him up to everything he was capable of.

As of now, the only time I'm not working is when I'm at the gym or during my weekly lunch meetings... sorry—*bachelor meetings*— with the guys, and that's only because Lawrence and Oskar physically dragged Ivor and me from our desks. Especially today, when my hair was still, despite numerous showers, coated with a fine sheen of glitter that wouldn't come out. My room looked like a damn Hobby Lobby.

But I wasn't like my father, as much as I wanted to be. Although I knew I wanted everything my father had, especially that all-encompassing love, I didn't have a family yet, and the closest thing I had to a relationship was with my job. Taking over the firm is still one of the proudest days of my life, and it felt great to see our firm grow every day.

"What is the name of this bakery again?" Oskar asks with a frown.

I check the text from dad. "'You Knead Sweets.' Apparently, my father goes every morning to get my mom one of their cupcakes but forgot to place an order for her birthday next week before he left town."

Excitement flits across Lawrence's face, "I know that place; their cupcakes are fucking amazing. I make a point to go there a few times a week. But my favorite desserts are the chocolates Betsey makes. Now that I think about it, I'll grab a few when we get there."

"Betsey?" I ask, eyebrow raised and entirely curious how he's on a first-name basis with the baker. Not that I should be surprised; Lawrence is, and always will be, a man whore. An upfront one, but a whore nonetheless.

"Yeah." He nods. "The bakery has been all over the news. Betsey bought the space, and almost overnight, it blew up. If it weren't for the fact that her desserts really are worth the hype, I would say it's because one of her best friends is Maeve Caley, who sometimes helps behind the counter. Although, I haven't had a chance to see her yet." His excitement would be endearing if I didn't recognize the look in his eyes. Interest. Though, by the way, he's practically salivating, he is more interested in the baked goods.

"Maeve Caley? The international supermodel Maeve Caley? Behind the counter? Must be quite a best friend," Oskar whistles. Ivor grunts in agreement. *Caveman*.

Once we arrive at the shop, it's practically overflowing with people outside, eating their treats with huge smiles. Oskar opens the door for us, and a crowd piles past us before we can enter. Even so, the place is immaculate—plush powder blue booths, with smaller tables and couches dotted around the ample space. Taking up most of the room are two separate wall-to-wall displays full of sweets and baked goods. My eyes widen; the sheer number of desserts is mind-blowing. It was downright incredible that one woman created all of this. I stare as the staff seamlessly move around each other like a well-oiled machine, quick and efficient in their actions, almost as if they were performing a ballet.

"Impressive," I say out loud to the others.

"Wait until you try the sweets," Lawrence adds, his face smeared against a window display like a child.

"Hey! Tall, dark, and Armani, do not press your face against the displays. I just disinfected them." A husky voice, heavily accented, comes from behind the counter, followed by a curvaceous woman popping up from behind, a scowl on her beautiful face.

"Tall?" Oskar raises an eyebrow.

"Dark?" I question.

"Armani?" Ivor rakes his gaze over Lawrence. "*That* suit is Alexander Amosu."

We turn as one to look at Ivor, and he shrugs with a sigh. "Don't look so surprised. I'm a suit snob. You all know this."

"You're wearing a suit worth almost *one hundred grand* to a bakery?" a voice scoffs and up pops another gorgeous woman, this time a redhead, from behind the counter. Maeve Caley. I blink; she is even more striking in person.

"Who is? Is he part of the mafia? Is he coming for cupcakes for *La Famiglia*?" Another voice joins the other two as a blonde-haired vixen pops up. She laughs throatily as she attempts to mimic an Italian accent terribly.

Maeve scoffs, "no, I can spot mafia a mile away."

The blonde vixen rolls her eyes and looks at me, her eyes roaming my body, then laughs. "Why is your hair covered in red glitter?" The ladies share a look and give each other a small smile.

"Some prank... can we ignore the glitter-infested PTA mom-wannabe and the fact that the counter just became a hot girl version of whack-a-mole? Let's rewind to the handsome comment," Lawrence smiles, and I watch with amusement as he turns on his charm. Poor girl doesn't stand a chance.

She shrugs, "I also call you *pendejo*," she adds, and Ivor chokes in response.

Lawrence peers over at him with a raised brow. "What? What does that mean?"

"It means stupid," she answers for Ivor.

"What? Why?" He asks, his face turning incredulous. I think he's struck silly at the thought of a woman not falling for him when he hits them with *the sex charm*, as it calls it. But I am here for it.

She rolls her eyes, her accent rolling off her tongue, "maybe because you come in here three times a week with a different woman on your arm each time..." she pauses before adding, "You're a *puto*, you know."

"Wait, I know that one. I am not a whore," he says, his head rearing back as he clutches his chest.

"TotallyAWhore," Oskar coughs into his fist.

"DickDipper," I cough into mine.

Lawrence glares at us, shaking his head. Ivor completely ignores the exchange, instead having a stare-off with the model. *What the fuck is that about?*

"What would you call it, then?" She asks with a low growl.

"Equal Opportunity, sweets and baked goods, shopping." Lawrence grins, and she scowls, popping down and walking away.

"What did I say?" he holds his hands up, palms up, his eyebrows scrunched.

"Wow, you *really* are a Grade A, dumb-ass," I laugh, clapping his back.

"Grade F is more like it. Was that an actual attempt at hitting on someone? Telling them, you're an equal opportunity shopper? Like a bargain shopper?" her friend shakes her head with a scoff, "I would feel bad for you, but at least you have a nice warm hundred-thousand-dollar suit to keep you warm at night. Maybe... if you stroke the label and whisper sweet nonsense into the label, like call it a bargain suit, it will tickle your taint for you," the blonde jumps down from behind the counter with a laugh.

Oskar stares at her intently, a faraway look on his face, "I feel like I've seen her before."

Maeve looks away from Ivor and turns back to us, "you probably have. Lia is the best-selling realtor in the state. She has billboards everywhere. And you, sir," she points at Lawrence, who is still staring after the Latina, stars in his eyes. "You stay away from our Kati; she will skin you alive, and then we will have to close the bakery down for the day to hide the body. And you," she points at me next. "Don't get glitter on the baked goods," she tries and fails to hold back a smile. "Also, the line is moving. I suggest you move ahead." she pops down and walks through large swinging doors that must lead to the kitchen.

"I'm in love," Lawrence says softly, looking up at me with a puppy dog expression.

I roll my eyes, "shut up; You're not in love. You're in shock."

"You saw how she shut me down and called me out? It's been so long since anyone saw past my bank account," Lawrence says, almost absentmindedly.

I step forward with a chuckle, "what are you talking about? My mom called you a useless fridge raider just yesterday."

Lawrence rolls his eyes, neck craning for another look.

Oskar laughs and pats Lawrence's shoulder, "yeah, I don't think Mr. Charming here has ever been shut down when he hits them with the super smile. Kati is just what our man here needs."

I roll my eyes as Oskar cranes his neck, mirroring Lawrence's posture as he looks behind the counter. "What about Lia, her friend? I knew her face was familiar, one of the top realtors in Dallas. Her name floats around quite a bit; corporate heads flock to her when they want to find property in Texas, not just in Dallas. A smart woman who's made a name for herself - that sounds like someone I'd love to get to get to know better." He lets out a whistle in appreciation. "She's definitely right up my alley."

Ivor grunts, "That redhead is...interesting."

I whistle, "Wow, Ivor. That was, pretty much, a proposal coming from you. Look at us; we go to a bakery and end up on an episode of Ricki Lake and Steve."

I ignore their scowls and turn. Thankfully, I'm next in line.

I barely bite back a groan as I realize I am standing behind a guy trying— and failing— to shoot his shot with the woman at the register.

Jesus, I can't get away from the thirst today. My eyes flit around the room, half expecting to see little cupids flying around. I'd punch a little winged fucker in the face at this point. I don't want to waste time in some warped infatuation. Eventually, I will have the real thing.

My ears tune in to the conversation as I glance at my watch, planning to tell the guy to try again later because I am starving.

"Betsey, Betsey," he tsks, "don't worry about it. She's just a little girlfriend. It's not even that big of a deal. Besides, you and I both know that I rocked your world," the guy says with a sly grin, crossing his legs and leaning on the counter in a way that he probably thinks is sexy, but appears to be an attempt not to shit his pants.

Betsey, who I suppose was the famous owner, narrows her eyes at him.

"That's it." She smacks her hand on the counter, and her lip curls. "I was trying to remain professional in my place of business, but obviously, that isn't going to be possible. So, since you clearly need to hear this, let me tell you a little about yourself, Larry. Number one, you didn't rock shit, not even the bed, let alone my world. You lasted two pumps," she held her fingers up. "Count them! One, two. I wasn't even sure we were having sex yet, and then you passed the fuck out. You were snoring before you even rolled off me. I was still wearing half of my outfit, for fucks-sake. Number two, what in the fucking hell is a 'little' girlfriend? There was a bedazzled happy third-anniversary frame on your bedside table. Do you know how long it takes a woman to bedazzle? Let me tell you…it takes too fucking long. Especially for a man who shows up at a woman's bakery twice a day *begging* for a date when he should have been using his time to brush up on some Kamasutra. That way, he would be rocking his girlfriend's world instead of eating cookies. You," she digs her finger into his chest in rapid succession, "are a disgusting little man. Leave, and don't come into my bakery ever again. However, do tell your girlfriend she is welcome here anytime because any woman that has to put up with you in the bed deserves a fucking lifetime supply of chocolate." Her chin juts up, face bright red, chest heaving; she points at the door.

The guy stands there, mouth gaping, not realizing all the phones are pointed at him, recording the entire interaction. Lawrence included. I push his hand down and take the phone off him. Although I'm sure this little interaction will end up viral on social media, we weren't going to be the ones to post it. I can see the headlines now, "You Knead Sweets Bakery Owner, Kneads Proper Loving From Another Oven." "Kneads Sweets, Kneads a Good Man." "Bakery Owner, Kneads Help Filling *Her* Cream Puffs." Okay. Maybe not the last one, but still.

Over it, I tap his shoulder. "Okay, shit-head, you heard the lady. Time to go," I say, snapping him out of his stupor.

"Who do you…." he starts before turning. His words trail off as he looks up into my eyes and then at the equally imposing men behind me, and then back at me…again. We all had about a foot of height on him, all of us well over six feet, and thanks to the gym, we filled out our tailored suits very well. Add Ivor's hard look that promised death, and we were not easily dismissed or ignored.

His face pales, "I'll…uh…just…go…" Turning, he bolts out the door to the laughter of anyone watching, and it was quite a few people.

"You fucking go, girl!" Lia comes up behind her, fist-pumping. My head tilts as I register that Lia's voice sounds remarkably familiar, and I take a moment to look at her, but it just doesn't come to me.

Shaking my head, my attention snaps towards the owner as she opens her mouth. My eyes roam as I entirely drink in her beautiful pouty lips, bright with red lipstick and the wisps of black hair curling around her face, escaping from the tight bun at the top of her head. Add in an apron, heavily dusted in flour, which does nothing to hide her generous chest or slim waist, and I salivate. Finally, my gaze locks with a pair of light green eyes, and I feel a jolt of electricity in my chest, and my mind goes blank; although I know she is speaking, nothing registers.

"Are you okay?" I hear her ask, and Lawrence chuckles behind me.

I close my eyes briefly, mentally wipe the saliva from my chin, snap back into reality, and sigh, *fucking cupid and his butt fucking arrows*. But I knew this was more than cupid...this was fate.

Chapter Six
...LIKE A MYSTICAL FORCE...

Betsey

I ignore the phones pointing at me and take a deep breath as Larry leaves the store. The absolute fucking nerve of that piece of shit. Trying to gather myself, I look at the next person in line and almost pass out as that well-earned breath shoots back out of my lungs like a rocket on speed. Tall, dark, and with hair covered in red glitter. What are the chances…did he know it was us? Is that why he and his friends are here? I discreetly wave my hand behind me, urging Lia and Maeve to get to the back. He may not recognize me, but all four of us together? I wasn't taking that chance.

"Hello! Welcome to 'You Knead Sweets!' What sweets do you need today?" I ask and avoid making eye contact, lest he sees the truth in my eyes. Though, I shouldn't have worried because his face goes slack, and I raise my eyes in confusion and watch as his eyes go soft, taking on a glassy look as he slowly looks me up and down. My blood heats at the sheer hunger of his perusal as if he was trying to memorize my every feature. His gaze is almost physical, and I am suddenly aware of my heartbeat as shivers work their way up my spine, sending currents of electricity from my head to my toes.

I shake my head, trying to clear the cobwebs because, flattering as his attention was, this was the same guy that we got revenge on just last night. I can't pretend otherwise, even if his perfect jawline, wavy hair, and gorgeous green eyes gave me the first set of real butterflies I've had in years. But, God, even his muscular physique was working the fuck out of his expensively tailored suit.

I felt my two alter egos, Petty, and Betty, pop up on my shoulder for the first time since college.

Petty- I mean, I wouldn't be opposed to an enjoyable time with THAT. I bet he would last more than two pumps.

Betty- Hello! His hair is covered in red glitter. The same glitter you made explode from his car vents.

Petty pouts, "I wish we could have seen that…"

Betty rolls her eyes, "technically, you did. But that's beside the point here. He is clearly a bad investment."

Petty- Doesn't mean you can't fuck him senseless.

I shake them off and try to speak again, "Are you okay?"

He jolts, "fucking cupid and his butt fucking arrows."

I blink, "Um, what?" His 'hotness meter 'will have to have the dial turned all the way down if he is unhinged. No dick is worth that level of crazy. What if he steals my thongs while I sleep… and wears them? No, thank you. I sigh internally…*it's always the hot ones.*

"Never mind," he rubs the back of his neck. "Sorry about that, I have to order my mom a…" he briefly looks down at his phone, "a cupcake bouquet."

I nod as I grab our order form, "okay. That's easy enough. What is the day and occasion, how many cupcakes are in the bouquet, what kind of cupcakes, and will you need this delivered, or will you be picking it up?

He pauses, his eyebrows coming together.

"Fuck, my dad didn't say," he sighs, running his hand through his hair. *Damn, so soft looking. I wonder what conditioner he uses. I wonder if he used that on his facial hair too.* Fuck me. He *is* stunning.

"Let me handle this," his friend pushes him out of the way and hits me with a smile that almost knocks me off my feet. I should be used to it by now. He's in here nearly three times a week, but no, he has that kind of smile that punches you in the vagina every time.

"Hi, I'm Lawrence, but I guess you know that. He will take a varied flavor bouquet of 100 cupcakes. To start, can you include at least ten of those victoria sponge cake style cupcakes, raspberry filled, with praline frosting? Oh, and at least ten of your carrot cake cupcakes with the butter walnut cream filling and walnut cream-cheese frosting. Oh, Oh! At least a few of your chocolate cupcakes with that mouth-watering chocolate whiskey filling with the whiskey-whipped frosting?"

I write quickly as Lawrence claps his hands, his eyes almost feral as he trips over his words, "Also, momma Weild *definitely* has to have your red velvet cupcakes with Jamaican Rum cream cheese frosting... Can you add those little squeezy plastic tubes filled with the rum on the top too? Then, of course, we need to throw in those hazelnut crème brûlée style cupcakes with the crunchy top. Those are so fucking good. Oh, how about those hummingbird cupcakes? The Pineapple banana ones with that special pineapple cream cheese frosting? Hmm," he pauses in thought. "Let's top it off with your special champagne cupcakes with the light strawberry cream filling paired with your extra whipped, buttercream frosting. You know what? Better make that 200 cupcakes." He nods rapidly.

My mouth hangs open slightly, and I burst out with laughter. I share a look with Mr. Red Glitter, and he shrugs his shoulders with a wide grin.

"What he said," he laughs, sliding me over a sleek, heavy,

black card with no name or numbers. Well damn, if the suit and smell of money pouring off him wasn't a clear indicator, he is certainly well-off.

"Dude, you spend way too much time here," one of his friends shakes his head at Lawrence while the terminator-looking one grunts in agreement.

"No such thing as too much time at You Knead Sweets bakery. I would sleep in the kitchen if I could, sneaking crumbs." His face takes on a wistful expression.

"Well, at least that redeems you a bit, *pendejo*." Kati chimes in helpfully from behind me.

"Does that redemption get me your number?" Lawrence flashes another panty-melting smile, hearts in his eyes.

"Not a chance," she scoffs, turning on her heel, her hips swaying as she enters the kitchen.

"I am going to marry that woman. Mark my words." Lawrence rubs a palm over his heart, almost looking like he is about to jump over the counter to be near her.

I scoff, not wanting to break his heart, and turn back to Red Glitter with my professional face on. "Okay, no problem. What day do you need them delivered?"

"Her birthday party is next week Saturday, so that is... February 7th by 11 am?"

I quickly figure out the logistics in my head. It's a lot of different cupcakes, but it can be done. "That works." I charge his card, pass him his receipt, and get the address notated.

"Before I forget, here is my number. In case you need to reach me for any changes or...anything else."

His voice goes several octaves lower, which startles me, and my eyes clash with his heavy gaze. I reach out with trembling fingers, and he casually caresses my wrist as he places it in my hand. I feel another current of electricity jolt through me and I resist the urge to check under the counter for a loose wire as my throat thickens. *What in the fucking Pikachu was this?* I think to myself.

His left eyebrow raises a fraction before he gives me a smile that speeds my pulse. I place the card into my pocket without looking at it, even though I want to. At least to put a name to the face instead of 'Red Glitter Man.'

Lawrence breaks the rising tension by slapping him on the shoulder. "If I can't make a love match, I'm not letting you make one. Bro-code man. Now, time for the good stuff." He shuffles on his feet. "Before we go, I'll have a dozen of whatever cupcake special of the day you have and three pounds of your hazelnut toffee truffles." He slaps an identical card on the counter.

I can't help but chuckle at his enthusiasm as I get his order ready. Except, my focus wavers as my eyes continuously seek 'Red Glitter,' and his gaze is fixated on me each time. I try to breathe, the air thick as I move faster, needing him out of my bakery. His intensity is a strange combination of unsettling and thrilling, flushing warmth throughout my body. It makes it hard to think, and I try to remember why I can't just grab him and make him my next tasty project.

Betty pops back up to whisper, 'Betsey. It's because he was a target of revenge just last night. He is not a target for passionate sex.'

'Argh, I'm just saying... unhand me, you heathen!' Betty yells as Petty pops in, grabs her in a chokehold, and drags her back into whatever parallel universe they live in.

My mouth goes dry at the thought of passionate sex, and I avert my gaze as I pass Lawrence his boxes with a quick thank you.

Like a mystical force, my head snaps when the door chimes and my eyes are drawn to his like a magnet.

Leaning against the door, his eyes gleam, "I look forward to seeing you again, Betsey." As he saunters out of the shop, his voice is a smooth, dark promise.

"Lady, if you don't call him... I will take out my false teeth and swallow him down faster than sinners chug that Sunday wine," a voice comes from the other side of the counter.

A laugh rings out in the bakery, and I shake my head at one of the regulars, Gladys, a 70-year-old grandma who comes in weekly for treats for her grandchildren. Although, as spritely as she is, you'd never know her age.

"Gladys, you are married!" Lia chimes in, marching out of the kitchen now that the men have walked out of the store.

She scoffs, "I'll take my usual dear," she directs at me before looking back at Lia, fanning her face. "Chile! Did you see those men? I would start one of those... What do you call them? Oh, reverse harems. My Harold will just have to make some space on the bed. I had my hips replaced a few years ago; I can keep up with the young ones."

I choke on my spit and wheeze a laugh, "Here is your order, Gladys. I will see you next week."

"If you're having trouble swallowing, I know a great...."

I cut her off with a laugh, "bye, Gladys!"

She cackles as she walks out of the shop with a wave.

"Got to admit, *amiga querida*, Grandma Gladys knows how to get down," Kati giggles.

"Yeah, clearly," I mutter as I turn to the next customer. *This day just got a lot longer.*

Petty appears back up on my shoulder, legs crossed as she rubs on her horns suggestively, licking her lips, *"like his thick cock! Because let's be real. You know that man is packing something serious."*

I stop myself from rolling my eyes and brush her off, his card burning a hole in my pocket.

Chapter Seven
...CUPCAKE BANDITS, FOREVAH, BITCHES!...

Betsey

The days pass in a blur, and we don't get any more 'Petty Betty' business, which annoys the others. I know this because Lia won't shut up about it. According to her, she's managed to grab some awesome costumes inspired by our very first job. I know better than to ask her, and she's remaining suspiciously quiet about it.

Which coming from my mouthy friend, is very worrying.

But I haven't had time to think about it too much. The shop has been busier than usual, and with making all the cakes for the bouquet, I'm a bit frazzled. After a couple of callouts, I was fortunate that Maeve still hadn't left for Maui and that Lia was also helping. I was going to have to hire more staff because, as it was, we were so busy it was hard to breathe. I certainly needed another baker.

"Hey, you have another delivery of flowers boss. Do you want me to set them up around the bakery like all the others?" Leanne, one of my best pastry helpers, pops her head into the kitchen. I nod and she bustles off.

I throw my head back with a sigh. That was another thing;

the day after Red Glitter man, whose name was Nathan, I started receiving bouquets of roses. Not just one or two roses, but one-hundred roses a day, the kind that made your entire house smell like a damn garden. Every message said the same thing; I'll *wear you down eventually; until then...these roses are almost as sweet as you. 786-555-5555.*

Since then, I've been taking his card out of my desk and staring at it. Contemplating if I should call the number. I admit my resistance was waning.

Maeve finds me in the kitchen, where I'm covered in flour. "More flowers from Mr. Glitter? Sounds like he isn't backing off; maybe you should call him."

She laughs at my eye roll. "Anyways, someone's asking for another bouquet this week. Can you? They're not worried about flavor, so maybe we can do more of the ones you had planned?"

I huff a breath and swipe my arm over my forehead. "Yeah, not a problem; I'll do it."

"Awesome. Thanks, babe," she gives me one of her grins that can cause a car crash and whirls out, her hair a streak of fire behind her. After that, it's not too hard to adjust the quantities, and I sigh contentedly as I slide back into the familiar rhythm. My kitchen, covered in flour and baking treats, is my favorite place to be, and I'm not ashamed to say that Maeve being out front helps bring more people in. Fortunately, she likes it well enough, or rather, she loves me too much to say otherwise. We like to joke that it forces her to practice the sweet side of her sour-patch kid personality.

Regardless, she does better than Kati does at the front since Kati prefers to serve our sweets with an extra side of '*no me joda,*' as she likes to say.

Speaking of. Kati comes in like a tornado, chattering wildly as she looks down at her phone. She curses and slams it down on the counter with an ominous crack. Although, miraculously, she still held on tightly to her cup of expresso without spilling it. Magic.

"Motherfucking biscuit whore. *Maldito hombre del carajo*," she seethes, accent thick, pacing the floor like a cornered animal.

"Well, that's a new one," I say lightly while laying out my cupcake trays. "Everything okay?"

She scowls, "No. Here I was, trying not to cuss too much, but fuck it. That will never work."

"Riiiight. So, what's going on?"

She prowls over to the delicate tarts I made earlier and swipes three in quick succession. "So, I got another job for Petty Betty. Not through the site, but I witnessed it first hand." She takes another two.

I dust the flour onto my pants and then wait with crossed arms, "what happened?"

She motions at me to wait as she finishes chewing. "*Mira*, so here I was down the street minding my own business...."

"Meaning you were people-watching while drinking another expresso from the Latin restaurant two blocks away. Seriously, Kati, that *cafecito* is your fourth this morning alone." I shake my head in awe.

"Well, if you would get *un maldito* expresso machine, I wouldn't have to sneak out and get one. Also," she waves her hand, "how many times do I have to tell you that I'm Puerto Rican and Dominican? We drink coffee from the breast at birth. Bustelo is equal to Similac; expresso doesn't affect us the same way. *Es como agua!*"

I roll my eyes, "If it were like water, you wouldn't be so jittery."

"Bah, *no me joda*. Can we get back to my anger, please?"

I hide a smile and nod, mixing while she vents.

"So, like I said, minding my own business. There was a woman with a sweet little boy who couldn't be more than two years old in a screaming match with some *cabrón, una concha de su madre*. Next to her was a pregnant woman in tears. From what I got, this guy has been in a relationship with her and this other woman for years. She found out because of the other woman, the pregnant one, although I wouldn't be surprised if there were more at this point. Anyways, the pregnant lady reached out to her when she found his hidden phone. She was holding the phone in his face showing him the proof. The sad part is that the little boy is also his." She's so angry that it's a struggle for her to get the sentences out. "This is why I *fucking* hate men and the reason I will always stay single. *Eso malditos* just put their dick in everything; they never want to stick to one person. Whatever happened to loyalty, commitment, love?" She shakes her head, eyes burning with rage.

I wish I had an answer for her—shit, for all women. The truth was, love was hard enough by itself, opening yourself up to someone and the possibility of being hurt. Let's not even get started on trying to date in the age of tinder and all these dating apps that are just magnets for hookups. Add in social media, bogged down with people who post fairy tales instead of reality and, anyone can feel inadequate. I wasn't opposed to finding love, but I *was* opposed to the bullshit it took to get to the happy ending. Conflicting emotions, but there it was.

"After he left, I walked up and told them Petty Betty was exactly what they needed. I gave them the website info. But in that fucker's case, we will need a bit more than just petty. We are going to have to get *really* close to possibly going to jail," her eyes almost feral as she bounces on her feet, taking several bites of the pastries. Indeed, it was impressive how she could talk, drink and still savagely attack her food.

Lia bustles in at that point, her arms full of shopping bags. "The bakery smells like delicious pastries and roses. I am impressed he hasn't let up. Anyways, look what I got on... oh. What's going on here? Why's Kati attacking the pastries as if they've offended her?"

Kati drinks her coffee, her face icy, "Some *pendejo* thinks he can lead a double life, family and all, and Petty Betty is going to rain down fire on his ass." Kati crosses back to me, away from the food, hands on her hips. "Betsey, do you mind if we do a freebie on this one? Consider it a family referral?"

"Sure. I mean, considering the ten grand we got from the last person, I think we are okay with a few freebies. Besides, it's not like we need the money; it was just to weed out the fakes," Lia cuts in, eyes sparkling before I can say anything. "An asshole like that can't go unchecked. So it's down to Petty Betty to bring him down." She drops the bags with a loud 'whoop,' high-fiving Kati.

Their excitement is contagious, and I join in, "cupcake bandits, forevah, bitches!" I cry in my best warrior impression, grabbing my spatula and thrusting it into the air.

There's a beat of silence, and we break down into fits of laughter, and Maeve comes back in with a grin.

"Did I hear Betsy shouting about cupcake bandits? Did I come in just in time for some revenge planning? No details needed; I need some action before I leave for Maui." She says, leaning against the worktop next to Lia. "Oooh, a nice haul of shopping," she says, peering into the bags.

"We will get to whatever shit Lia buys later; I am afraid even to know what's in those bags anyway. But, we need to plan this shit," Kati grabs a pen and slaps a napkin down forcefully. "The glitter squad, cupcake bandits, and petty betties are in session."

Maeve snorts. "Are you seriously going to write on that? Don't we need matching planners or a petty secretary?"

Kati groans and waves her pen in the air. "Nope. No evidence; we can wipe our asses with this after. Let's carry on!"

We blink, then shrug. She has a point. It can't get any more villainous than using your written plans as toilet paper.

"Alrighty then," Lia claps her hands and gives her best Ace Ventura impression. "Who has ideas to add to our portfolio? I have some ideas. Like breaking in and stealing one sock, they have a load of uneven socks." She throws her head back with a cackle.

Kati gives her throaty chuckle. "Fuck no. We can add that to something, but this *testa di Cazzo* will need something a little more...uncomfortable."

"Oooh, going a little Italian, are we?" Maeve grins. "I like it."

Kati taps her pen on the napkin. "Sparkle up my cupcake bandits. We have an act of revenge to plan."

Chapter Eight
...I NEVER LOSE...

Nathan

"Hey man, the Ardini brothers are here; Tiffany is leading them into the meeting room. You ready to crush this meeting?" Lawrence strides into my office like he owns the damn place, his signature smile on his face. Oskar is hot on heels, a gleam of excitement in his eyes, and throws himself into one of my chairs.

Chuckling, I lean back in my chair and shake my head at their animated faces. They live for meetings. Though I admit, I also love the rush of closing a deal, and this one, in particular, will be a significant opportunity for the Weild firm. The Ardini Architecture firm, owned by brothers Eason and Wilder, is one of the biggest and most lucrative firms in New York City, and they plan to expand to the Dallas market. As if that wasn't enough for us to have a meeting with them, the Ardini brothers plan to split their interests to match both markets, so, in effect, Weild will oversee two separate multi-billion-dollar portfolios.

"I do not doubt that this meeting will go well. Do we ever lose?" I stand and straighten my suit.

"I don't know, man; Betsey still hasn't taken the bit," Lawrence teases.

"I think you've sent about 700 roses. Is our Nathan losing his touch?" Oskar exchanges a knowing look with Lawrence.

Except they don't know shit. I wasn't sure what it was about that woman, but I knew she was mine the moment I met her. My father always said that the Wield men intuitively knew their soulmate; it was our family's benediction, our blessing. I always jokingly called bullshit, even though it was clear that he and my grandfather were deliriously infatuated with their wives.

Me? I was infatuated with my work and dedication to growing the firm, and it was because I knew there was no point in picking up my head until I met the person meant for me, *my Weild woman*. Dates and flings were just to fill a primal need; they all knew the score. But Betsey? She is mine; she didn't realize it yet.

I shook my head as they carried on, ignoring them as I grabbed my materials for the meeting before I stride over to the window to look down at the bustling financial district. While Weild owned the entire high-rise building, our offices and conference rooms were at the top. It was always a favorite place of mine to play when my father had this office. I was knee-deep in investment banking between his office and my mother's. I grew up hearing all the meetings from my playpen, and then when I learned how to walk, I would sit in my father's lap. When I got restless, I would go down to the massive nursery that took up an entire building floor. Weild was a family-oriented firm, and my mother and father ensured it was known.

I turn and look fondly around the room, as I often did before any meeting, to remind myself how important this firm is to me and why I will always acquire every deal that will benefit our firm. The room is very spacious and elegantly decorated, with floor-to-ceiling windows that offer a stunning view of the city. The walls are lined with bookshelves filled with leather-bound books, various awards, and achievements. My desk, the same desk my father sat behind for 20 years, is large and imposing, made of dark mahogany wood. The only difference now was my state-of-the-art computer, instead of the ancient desktop. The seating area consists of plush leather armchairs and a matching couch, where Lawrence and Oskar were currently draped on like savages, with a low-lying coffee table made of glass and steel. The overall aesthetic exudes power and success, something the Weild Firm prides itself on.

I smile because my office will eventually have a playpen where my son or daughter would hang out with their dad. It's been an almost obsessive thought since I met Betsey, and I always get what I want.

"Okay, let's go." I stride to the door, knowing that Lawrence and Oskar will follow.

Wilder (This is Important! Promise! Keep Wilder in mind)

Eason and I share a knowing look as Weild and his two partners, Burke and Palmer, enter the conference room simultaneously. It's a move Eason, and I have perfected; the show of confidence and power. It was effective; as was the posh conference room with wall-to-ceiling windows offering stunning views, a sizeable gleaming mahogany table in the center surrounded by high-end leather chairs. The walls were adorned with expensive art pieces and a simple canvas with 'Weild' in the center. The message was clear; there was no need to display the company's various accolades, which they certainly had plenty of, because they were simply the best.

It was why Eason and I had already decided to go with their

Investment Firm. There is no competition, the best required the best, and we were the best.

Nathan

As we enter the room, the Ardini brothers stand, and we exchange firm handshakes and introductions.

We take our seats at the table, and I smile, "I see my assistant, Tiffany, has already passed out our proposals. As you can see, our relationship can potentially bring in significant returns for Ardini Architecture Firm."

Wilder laughs, "relationship, huh? A little presumptuous, is it not?"

I give a chuckle of my own, "not at all. I know smart businessmen when I see them. Ardini Architecture Firm is the best firm in New York. With you expanding into Dallas, there is only one obvious choice to ensure your success."

"Seems like it would certainly be mutually beneficial, no?" Eason leans back in his chair.

Oskar gives an easy smile, his eyes sharp, "absolutely. Your firm, as you well know, has a great reputation. Combining our resources will bolster that. Weild doesn't align itself with just anyone."

"But before we get to the inevitable signatures," Lawrence smirks, "let's go over a few details. What are your goals for developing the new building and the budget parameters?"

Wilder leans forward on his elbows, "we have already contacted the best real estate agents and set up a meeting. I'm sure you've heard of her, A Ms. Lia Oliver?"

Oskar sits up a little straighter in his seat, eyes brighter, and I hide a smirk. Ever since he met Lia, he has been trying to figure out a way to see her organically. While I was much more of an aggressive pursuer, Oskar wanted to make it all natural.

With Ardini using Lia as their real estate agent, Oskar, our firm liaison, would also have to meet with her.

At our nod of acknowledgment, Wilder continues, "After we acquire a location for our office, our initial project will be a mixed-use development in the heart of the city. We're looking to build luxury condos, high-end retail space, and boutique hotels in various locations within Texas, not just Dallas. So our reach is wide, and the budget is substantial, but of course, we want to make lucrative investments that will bolster our portfolios over time to ensure we can continue to build and grow."

I nod, "we are on the same page there. We have provided you with a list of potential investment possibilities because while Ardini can be sure we will do what is best for the firm, we also believe in transiency."

Wilder's lips curl in a smile, and he nods at Easton. They both stand, "show us the dotted line. Ardini looks forward to working with Weild Investment."

Adrenaline floods my body at the familiar rush that comes with closing another deal.

I never lose, and Betsey will figure that out soon enough.

Chapter Nine
...AND THE OSCAR GOES TO...

Betsey

"This dress is so fucking short that you can see my shaving rash," Lia grumbles as she tugs the hem down of her dress.

"Quit acting like you don't wear this shit all the time," Kati slaps her hand away.

"You look like a model, and that's coming from one," Maeve grabs Lia's hands when she tries to readjust her dress. "Just be cool and give him one of these," she hands a small pill over, which Lia takes in the palm of her hand.

Her eyes bulge, mouth gaping, "I'm not about to roofie a guy. Not doing it." Lia tries to hand it back, and Maeve shakes her head.

"No, dumbass. This is just an herbal laxative. Something that dissolves in a drink. Make sure you put it in his water because if it is in his alcohol, he'll probably shit a lung out."

My laughter rings out, and all the girls look at me like I've lost the plot, but all I can picture is this guy on the toilet later, praying for it to stop. Is it a little dark for petty revenge? I don't think so. This guy deserves worse, to be honest. I mean, what sort of asshole has a double life so intricate that they have two families? Nope, fuck that noise. Situations like this are part of why we needed to start Petty Betty back up. It was our job to even the scales of Karma because, let's be honest here, sometimes that cunt takes too long.

So, after some digging on Tinder, —because why wouldn't this asshole have an active Tinder?— Kati pointed out the guy she saw in the street, Jordan. Lia set up a fake profile, swiped right, and within moments he swiped back, and that's all it took. Premium account much? It figures that this thirsty asshole is already searching for another conquest after being found out.

There's a small weight on my shoulders as Petty and Betty come out to play. Betty fluffs her wings before adjusting her halo, and Petty shines her horns before she hikes up her already short dress. Internally, I roll my eyes. My adorable self-admiring Id and Ego, folks.

Petty - I say we put the laxatives in his alcohol. What's the worst that can happen?

Betty - You heard Maeve. He could probably shit a lung out. How do you think the cops would feel if we told them, 'sorry, we only put a little bit of the laxative in the alcohol, but please feel free to reattach his lung?'

Petty scrunches her face;- *It's a figure of speech. He's not actually going to lose a lung. He's likelier to shit so much that his dick ends up dangling into shitty water.*

She cackles, eyes watering. Although, I must admit that it *is* an equally gross and entertaining image.

Petty- Also, consider it an act of goodwill, she grimaces, nose scrunching at the word 'good.' *It will kick start some weight loss, and besides, the fucker deserves it.*

Betty rolls her eyes;- *'Good' is not a curse word, you know? You should try it; sitting on a tail with a spike on the end must be difficult.*

Petty- As tough as fixing a fucking halo all damn day and fluffing your wings. How do you even sit on a chair with those things? Don't make me choke your fluffy ass out again!

Betty rolls her eyes with a fake yawn- Anyways. Ultimately, it's up to Lia. Not Betsey, so the point you're making doesn't matter. Thankfully.

Petty - But she could slip one in the drink as she walks by or can bribe the server to let her take the order—

Betty - Nope. No. Nada. Niete. However, you want to say it; the answer is no. Read my lips. N.O. Got it? Comprende? Too many variables, Petty.

Petty - Sheesh, you are no fun. I bet Kati would be on board with this and let me have at least a little fun.

Betty - Well, she might be a little saner than our Betsey. I haven't seen her Id and Ego hanging around. Betsey needs us; we help her ease her mind by doing this on the outside. Our banter hides her crazy, and that's the way we like it.

Petty - Careful, you're starting to sound a little naughty.

Betty - Oh, fuck off.

And with that, they poof from my shoulders, and I've missed Lia's entrance. We all pile into another table nearby with the women who decide to get their revenge on a video call. They have their own petty revenge planned for when this guy gets home, and I am so here for it.

"I feel like we should be in our masks again," Maeve whispers and giggles behind a menu the server gave her with a huge smile. "It seems so wrong to watch it play out without our uniforms. I feel exposed!"

"Ay, *callate coño*. The dude doesn't have any idea who we are. We're just three hot as fuck, women out for a nice meal and drink to celebrate our success. He doesn't have to know the success we are celebrating is his downfall." She gives her devilish smirk and flutters her hands at the guy sitting in the corner with a nervous-looking Lia.

"Voodoo priestess much?" I whisper.

"Nah, I'm not into the evil *Santeria*. Too much bad juju. I also don't have the time for chicken blood. I prefer old fashion shit," she casually takes a sip of her drink.

Maeve and I look at each other and shrug.

"We are just at the apartment now," one of the women, Sarah, says in a whisper. We look at the phone to see her and another woman next to her, faces solemn, nodding. I am happy they're sticking together in this situation; there is way too much blame culture on the women in these situations instead of the pieces of shit who have been leading double lives. They're going to be okay after this. I can feel it.

The server approaches their table, and the piece of shit guy places his hands over Lia's possessively and takes the menu off her, ordering for her. I roll my eyes; he was lucky Lia had a role to play. Otherwise, he would have had her foot up his ass.

He leans in to whisper in her ear, and Lia tosses her hair over her shoulder and gives him her boxer-dropping sexy smile. Lia shifts slightly and touches her hand to her chest with a laugh before reaching up to play with her hair coquettishly.

The server finally walks off, which is my cue to enter the kitchen to fulfill my part of the petty. It's no streak of luck that they're at this specific Michelin-star restaurant. I happen to know the head chef.

I pop my head through the doors, instantly transported to the days when I used to work in this environment before realizing pastries were my calling.

The man I'm looking for towers above everyone else, his face set in a scowl. To others, he's a scary motherfucker, a Caribbean version of The Rock. However, seeing as how I've known him since we were younger, he was just a cuddly, ginormous wall of muscle and one of my best friends. The type of person that would do anything for you once you earn their loyalty. I sigh internally; if he weren't gay, I'd marry him in a heartbeat, but alas, we both love the dick too much.

"Betty Boop, how are you, darling? I haven't seen you around for a while," he spots me, eating up the distance with his long strides, and engulfs me in one of his enormous hugs.

I laugh. If anyone else were to call me 'Betty Boop,' I would use their heart as an ingredient in one of my cakes. Still, our bond was cemented between the hours in culinary school and all the hours chugging wine while bonding over the mental images of tripping our instructors into a vat of lard. So, of course, he gets to use "Betty Boop" all he wants. Anyways, Dimitri is part of my family. My chosen one anyway, but most times, those were the most substantial kinds.

"Dee. My man. How are you? The place looks busy." Dimitri rolls his eyes with a small; I have special name privileges too, I boast...to myself...*jeez, lonely much in your head, Betsey?*

"Yeah, can't complain." He steers me out of the chaos and into his tiny office. "What can I do for you, however? You're all dressed up, and you have that look in your eye, so I know this isn't a social call."

A huge grin stretches across my face. "I promise we will get together for a social one soon. It's been crazy busy for us, but I have a favor to ask." My mind kicks into overdrive and adds, "and a proposition."

"Well. Color me intrigued. I'm listening hot stuff."

I snort at him and then say, "two words. Petty Betty."

"Who is she, and what has she done to you?" He's immediately on the defensive, ready to cut a bitch for me, and it just makes me love him that little bit harder."

"She's me. Well... if you want to get down to it, she's me, Lia, Kati, Maeve, and I was also hoping...you."

He bites his lip and then shuts the door, so we're entirely in silence. "Tell me more," he demands, hands rubbing together dramatically as he leans against his desk.

I laugh and clap my hands together, leaning forward into his personal space. "Let's say we have recently arranged a service to get... revenge against some exes or those who have taken advantage of, how do I say...the delicate sensibilities of scorned women."

His eyes sparkle, and his face melts into a beatific smile, "oh, honey, you had me at revenge," he snaps his fingers; excitement is written all over his gorgeous face.

"I knew you would be. Now," I lower my voice, even though the door's closed. "Are you ready for your first-ever mission?" He nods thoughtfully, and I catch him up to speed quickly.

"That son of a bitch needs to be castrated," he growls, eyes darkening. Dimitri had a rough start with his dad leaving his mom, him, and his brother for his *wife's* secretary. He couldn't even get his *own* secretary, asshole. He leans back against the wall, rubbing his chin, cogs turning.

His implacable expression is a bit alarming, and I place a hand on his huge bicep, "well, Honey Pot...."

He smirks, and I give a small laugh, "we're not going to jail for him, and he is going to get his karma," I soothe. "But I will need you to do something...culinarily painful for me, however. I need you to put a shit-ton of salt in his food. We need him to drink more."

He laughs, his eyes widening with understanding, "yeah, you want him to shit his pants. Don't worry; I got you, girl. While it will be painful for me to defile my masterpieces deliberately, no child deserves to grow up in a broken home, let alone see it unfold. So, let's do it."

I move towards the door but pause before I open it, something niggling at the back of my mind. "I don't think either one of them will be alone for too long. For one, they seem to be made of tougher stuff, and two, I've heard of a new dating agency that opened a couple of months ago. An acquaintance of mine opened one, so I'll pass on the details."

He looms behind me as I open the door. "Okay, Bets. Did you need anything else?"

"Nah, thanks, Dee. I'll come and speak to you later. When are you next off work?"

The noise hits me as we make our way back into the kitchen, all the people working efficiently and calling out instructions to one another.

"When am I ever off work, babe?" He scowls at one of the sous chefs, who drops a saucepan on the floor with a loud clatter. Sauce flies everywhere, and the kitchen seems to hold in a breath. That's my cue to leave, so I haul ass before heads roll.

Nothing has changed when I reappear at the table, except the ladies no longer on the voice call.

"Thank fuck you're back; I'm starving." Kati picks up her napkin and places it on her lap. "We ordered an appetizer and got you the house special main." She eyes up a server holding a basket of French Bread and olives like she's about to tackle him. "This better be for us," she mutters as he thankfully comes closer.

To everyone's relief, as a hangry, Kati is a dangerous one. So we tuck in while I get the updates on Lia and the fuck boy.

"She hasn't slipped him the pill yet. He's been so focused on touching her that she can't get a break," Maeve helpfully adds when I peek.

Sure enough, he's practically hanging over the table to remain in contact with Lia while she's almost balancing on her chair to get away from him. I've never seen her look so uncomfortable, and she can put up with a lot of shit, especially when dealing with sleazy corporate fucks looking for property. Unfortunately, this guy is a particular sort of an asshole.

"If she can't slip it, I'll handle it for her- with a fist to his nose. Then, I'll stuff the pill down his sleazy throat," Kati mumbles through a savage bite of her bread.

"Easy tiger." Maeve leans her head onto Kati's shoulder. "It will get done. But, for now, enjoy the food. It's my treat."

A crash comes from the table, and the guy jumps out of his chair, glancing down at his now soaking-wet top. His face darkens with anger, two bright red spots of pink on his cheeks, which I fixate on. He pastes a smile on his face, but underneath is a darkness that sends shivers down my spine; those women don't know it, but they are fortunate to have figured this asshole out sooner rather than later. My eyes flick towards Maeve, who has her eyes narrowed. Here's hoping our dose of revenge teaches him a lesson because I don't think he would survive the depths Maeve would be willing to go to punish an abuser.

"I am so sorry," Lia reaches over and attempts to dab at his top. "I'll grab you another water. I am so sorry."

He holds his hands up, and I miss what he says before he stomps toward the restroom. She sighs, shrugging her shoulders at us and glancing at the restroom door before running a weird shuffle over to our table.

"This guy, Jordan, is a pig." She runs a hand over her dress. "Honestly, all he's done this entire time is boast how successful he is in—wait for it— real estate."

"Oh, Shit." Kati throws her head back and laughs throatily, catching more than a few stares. "Does he know he's talking to the queen right now? Listed as the number one. 'Lease with Lia'? Is he for real?"

"Unfortunately." Lia takes another glance at the door. "I'm not sure how much more I can take of this guy. So, I 'accidentally' knocked his drink over and now need to put the pill in his water."

The door opens, and he wanders back to his table, doing a double take when Lia isn't in her seat. "Shit," she whispers before returning there and ensuring he's okay. They're right next to the bar, so I decide to help them along a little, grab the server who happens to be walking by, and point to Lia and Sir Twatwaffle.

"Hey, I noticed she knocked his drink over. I hate when dates don't go well. Can you ask the bartender to replace his drink and put it on my tab? I'll even walk over with you and take it to them myself; you look busy." I keep my voice soft and place a hand on her shoulder. She did look a little frazzled, and it works in my favor. All is fair in love and revenge.

The server smiles gratefully, "absolutely, thank you."

We make our way to the bar, and in minutes, I have a tray with a double Vodka on the rocks, a glass of water with ice, and a fruity cocktail for Lia. I make a show of going over to them, place the drinks down, and leaning close to him, my tits in my face. I quickly looked at Lia, ensuring she knew this was her chance.

"I saw what happened earlier with the drinks and decided to buy you some more. I'm doing a spiritual awareness course that strongly encourages me to do better things, which will manifest for me. So, I thought I would help you, which would then, in turn, help me in the future." I give him a bright smile and flip my hair over one shoulder.

As predicted, his sultry smile dims the more I speak, and his eyes glaze over when I start talking about spirituality. Lia nudges me on the ass, so I take that as my cue. "Well, enjoy your date." I give him one last bright smile for luck and saunter over to my table.

"I swear," Maeve states when I sit back down. "You have

been out of this chair more than in it today. You need to sit down and let Lia handle it."

"Well, she is. I just allowed her to hurry this shit along."

Now, we wait.

Their fancy entree appears, and we all take turns surreptitiously watching as he takes a mouthful, not seeming to notice extra salt. It makes me chuckle. Even when Dimitri is happy to help with the sabotaging, he will still make the food taste good. Sure enough, he reaches for a glass and takes a long swig, downing it in one.

"And we're a go for launch," Kati smacks her hand on the table.

We wait a little longer as they make small talk, or should I say; he talks to Lia while she nods and drinks her cocktail. But there is no sign of discomfort on his face. Then, we get a little nervous when the server clears the plates, and still nothing.

The guy reaches out and swigs the other drink on the table. He winces slightly and peers at the contents before finishing the rest in one big swallow.

"Now we're ready for launch," Maeve snickers, holds up her phone discretely and presses record on the video app.

And it really doesn't take long now that the ball, or pill, is in motion. He starts to adjust his collar, and even from here, you can see that the color of his face is now a sickly gray. He runs a hand through his hair several times and then snatches Lia's drink to place it at the back of his neck.

Suddenly, his chair skitters back and topples over. The noise draws the diners' attention, their faces all sporting matching expression that says, 'how dare someone interrupt my hundred-dollar caviar.' I bite back a smile as even the servers stop and stare in shock at the scene rapidly unfolding. Then, finally, he gives a pained cry and drops to the floor, curling in a fetal position—*great success,* I think, with a Borat voice.

"Call 911," someone shouts as gasps ring out around us.

My eyes widen; obvious that Lia has accidentally put the pill in his vodka rather than water. Kati is currently holding a trembling hand over her mouth, which, when I peer at her closer, the bitch is holding in laughter.

Suddenly Jordan screams, and a puddle of shit surrounds him. There's retching as people hustle to the doorway and sidestep the literal shit show.

Dimitri strides out from the back and puts on a show worthy of an Oscar.

"What has happened here? Why is he on the floor?" He demands.

A couple of people are still hanging around, the morbidly curious type—the curtain twitchers.

Lia fans herself and plays the concerned girlfriend. The guy doesn't even notice, too busy writhing around on the floor like a worm prostitute. Her voice shrill; Lia, vehemently shakes her head and puts her hands to her face, her eyes visibly watering.

With her body slightly turned to avoid the cameras, she does a weird sob-like scream, "Oh gods! He had a stomach issue but told me it was over, and that's why we came out. I never thought he would shit all over himself like this. I have no idea why he couldn't get to the bathroom in time."

Her eyes widen, and she covers her mouth with a gasp, "Oh no! Maybe...he did tell me he was suffering from weak sphincter muscles from all the toys we use, but it's been a few days since he's begged me to strap on for him. I've only had to put a collar on him, walk him around the room, and spank him. Oh no! Do you think the spanking made his sphincter worse? It was just the small paddle! Oh no! I broke his asshole! This is all my fault. I'm an asshole breaker!" She lets out a loud wail, furiously wiping at her face.

The few people, with their phones out, start laughing.

Dimitri visibly struggles, and his shoulders shake slightly, but he keeps his face blank, placing his hands on Lia's shoulder.

"Oh, my dear, I am sure *you* didn't break his sphincter. These things happen. You poor thing, it's going to be okay. Let's get you some water."

Lia continues to wail dramatically about being an anus destroyer as Dimitri leads her away, ignoring the guy on the floor with shit now coming out of the hems of his pants.

He takes a second to look back, "sir, this is a three Michelin Star restaurant, not a place for sphincter crises. I hope you know you will cover all bills accrued for disinfection and cleanup. Someone get this man a paramedic and a diaper." he tsks, nose scrunched, leading Lia away.

Jordan moans on the floor, completely oblivious.

"And the Oscar goes to," Maeve mutters and tucks her phone in her bag.

Kati giggles, falling over.

"Shit, Petty Betty strikes again. By tomorrow Lia would have made this asshole famous…Literally," I laugh as we stand up to leave the restaurant. Lia would meet us at the car, as planned.

We make sure not to get caught on screen on our way out, but everyone is too focused on the guy covered in his shit.

We giggle in the car as the ambulance crew turns up and clears him out; I can't help but chuckle when Kati jumps out of the car, raps her knuckles on the gurney, and says quietly. "You've been Petty Bettied, bitch."

Chapter Ten
...WHAT ARE YOU SCARED OF...

Betsey

The internet wins again. Just as we predicted, Jordan, now known as "The Rear Ranger," became a viral sensation overnight. The hashtag "Shit Show" was everywhere, trending on most social media platforms. The speed at which Jordan became a phenomenon was stunning, even attracting attention from celebrities who weighed in on the videos. Between TikTok videos, Instagram reels, Facebook videos, and Snapchat, the screenshots of his socials floating around, his face was the new, hot thing. The funniest ones are a little boomerang of him rolling in his shit. Fucking genius.

There's being the shit and being 'in' shit. This guy failed the assignment.
#FromPoopMaster to a #FecalGradePointAverage

Nothing says a shit show like rolling in it. #ShitShow #FecalFiasco

Is no one going to mention the rough spanking? #AnalDestroyer
#ShitShow #DefecationDemolitionist

Did you see his girlfriend? Think she wants someone with a stronger sphincter? I promise I won't turd into a #CrappyCasanova

Farts are not always your friend...Sometimes they are the start of #FecalFury #ShitShow

Defecation defect in full effect... #ShitShow

Alright, who stole the toilets? We are looking at you #BowelBullies #CrappyCrusadersStrikeAgain #PottyPirates #ToiletTerrors #RearEndRobbers

Did anyone see him pay for the meal? Quick, someone call the #TheShitSheriff to catch #TheFecalFelon #ThePoopBandit #TheCrappyCriminal

This guy's love life is officially over. He shit it to himself #Ex-Lax-ecutioner

That's a new way to dine and dash. Shit and ditch! #BowelBandit #TheTurdBurglar

You, sir, have betrayed all of us who can be pegged and hold our shit together. Literally. You will forever be the #RearEndRenegade

This is it folks...#TheCrappening! The culmination of all dad jokes that we dads have been waiting for. This is a total #BrownOut folks! The #TidesHaveTurds and the #TurdTornados are now approaching #Crap-egoryFive on the #SphincterScale. Simply put, this is the epitome of #NaturalDisasters...the #DiarrheaDisaster to be exact. Hunker down in the bathroom, folks. We must prepare to sit out this #ShitStorm.

The women also did a number on him by changing the locks so he couldn't get back into the apartment. Once he had, however, they had removed all his chargers and cords for his appliances. I'm going to have to remember that for another Petty Betty idea.

Not only did he become an internet sensation, but we may have leaked the story of his double life, and the internet thugs did the rest for us. The story hit the morning news as the new 'hot story,' and after they reached out to his job, a local bookkeeping firm, they advised that he was no longer with them as he did not fit their ideals—a fraud all around; no wonder he didn't recognize Lia.

We all have a spring in our step the following day, and I even manage to get up a little early and create a new cupcake recipe. Heavily inspired by yesterday's antics, it is a chocolate cupcake with an oozing hazelnut and a praline center with a hazelnut buttercream frosting. Topped with edible glitter, this was the official Petty Betty cupcake. I wanted to call it Glitter Shitter, but instead, I must opt for a 'Whole Lota Choca Glitter.'

My spring is even springy-er as today's roses from Nathan are delivered right before we open. Only this time, it is two-hundred roses, and the note changed. *'If I were to send a rose for every second you cross my mind, Dallas would be bereft of all its' petals. So instead, here are two hundred roses to cover the first two hundred seconds since I have opened my eyes. Forever yours (not that you know it yet), Nathan.* I swoon. I literally must hold on to the counter when I read the note.

Petty- I mean, honestly, I have nothing to say other than please call him and get us some dick.

Betty- No one will go through all of this for just a quick lay. He honestly seems sincere. Maybe that ex was unhinged? I mean, who pays that much money for an act of petty revenge, anyway?

Petty- Maybe his dick scrambled her mind. Forget her; I vote for a scrambling of our own. Call him.

Betty- If I agree with Petty, do I lose my angel wings?

I roll my eyes and brush them off, much to their discontent if the matching grumbles are any indication, and get back to my opening setup routine.

Lawrence enters the shop as I'm putting the new tray of cupcakes out, and he instantly makes a beeline for it. "A new cupcake. I'll take ten."

He looks around the bakery with a slight smile on his face. *Yeah, I'm getting your buddy's flowers.*

Before he can comment, Kati breezes out of the back and rolls her eyes when she sees him. "Ten? Have you upgraded the number of girls you see at once?"

Out of the corner of my eye, as I'm loading the cupcakes into a box for him, I see his smile vanish, wiped away by astonishment, "oh, you wound me. Since I met you, I've been a changed man." He tips me a wink when our eyes clash, and it takes everything in me to fight to remain neutral and not roll my eyes. Be professional.

Face slightly flushed, she eyes him with a calculating expression, "you were just in here last week with two different women, *baboso;* you changed so quickly?" She points at him, "your type will never be 'changed, men.' Once a man-whore, always a man-whore." She sashays over to the till and waits for me to pass the box before ringing him up.

He pauses for a moment, his dark blue eyes piercing the distance between them. I watch with a small smile as Kati raises her face to his and visibly swallows.

He leans against the counter, and his voice takes on a serious tone, "I resent that, you know. I'm 32, single, and if I'm not in the office, I am here getting Betsey's delicious treats. All those women you see me with are spoiled rotten but still understand that I am not... was not..." He corrects and looks at her pointedly before continuing, "looking for anything serious. There is nothing wrong with dating around."

He taps his card to the reader without looking at the amount, eyes firmly on Kati's face. "Nothing wrong with exploring my options."

Kati clears her throat and shoves the box into his chest, and I can see we need another little chat on how to remain professional and calm even when you want to knee people in the balls.

I stare, fascinated, as Kati goes quiet, and they lock gazes for what feels like an eternity, the electricity between them almost palpable. Petty speaks from my shoulder; *this must be what it looks like when animals meet in the wild*. Betty pops in; *I admit I may not want our Kati with this guy, but how he looks at her... woah*. I must agree with both. Because wow.

Kati breaks the stare off first, chin lifted and her accent suspiciously thicker, "the only thing you need to explore is an STI clinic. *Ahora, vete*! Bye, have a momentous day." She places one hand on her cocked hip and waves him off with another.

"You know, I've got a subscription to duo-lingo now...to try to learn as much Spanish as possible, in the hope that I can understand the insults hurled my way, but you know...they don't have an insult version of Spanish on the app. So, I suppose I will have to spend a lot more time around you to pick it up. Eventually, those insults will turn into praises. I'm going to break down your walls, Kati."

His appreciative gaze roams over her figure before returning to her face, "There is something about you that I plan to discover. Even if it takes the rest of my life, I just wanted you to know that when to get to know the real me...and you will... you will be surprised. I can tell you want to, no matter how much you protest. So, the real problem here is, what are you scared of?" He taunts, seeming to enjoy her struggle to capture her composure. Shit, I was too.

She grits her teeth, not responding, her face slightly dazed.

He chuckles, voice deep, dripping in promise. "I'll be

waiting for that answer. Until then, thank you for the cakes." He backs out the door with a devastating grin.

Kati's back turns ramrod straight before shaking her head, wiping the glazed look out of her eyes. "*Si el cres que me vas a cojer te tonta, con su seducion y ojos tan lindo...maldito.*"

I laugh, "to be fair, his eyes and smile are just downright seduction personified, so I don't think he is using that to seduce you. I have no idea whether he is trying to play for a fool. But damn, the chemistry between you two might have made me pregnant." I say to her.

She scoffs and waves her hand, "bah! It doesn't matter; I will not be taken prisoner by any man or his penis energy... and to prove it, I charged him a little extra for those special cupcakes. So now he won't think there is anything special other than shaky fingers," she cackles briefly before frowning, "Although I doubt he will even notice."

My jaw drops, "You didn't! You little shit! Kati, this is my business, don't start taking out your anger on the customers, or we may not have any."

"*Calmate*, Relax. It wasn't that much; consider it an asshole tax. Besides," she gives me the side-eye while fixing the cupcake display. "Even if he wasn't sending you hundreds of flowers, don't think that because we never mentioned it, we all didn't notice the eye sex you and Nathan had a few days ago. Or that you keep looking at his card that you have locked in your desk. So, if anyone is going down the sexual tension rabbit hole, it's you. Just call him. You need a night of mind-numbing sex instead a night of dreaming up recipes."

"Nice diversion..." I say drolly.

"Diversion or fact?" she smirks.

I roll my eyes as one of my regulars comes in with a warm smile that reminds me so much of my father that it is impossible not to match his exuberance. My mood brightens instantly, "Russell! I haven't seen you in a week. Your wife didn't need her Knead fix?"

Russell often stays behind to chat, and it is impossible not to love him. From my first dance recital, my dreams, and my goals, Russell knew it all. And while I won't admit it out loud, not seeing his face this week unsettled something in me. I started looking at him as sort of a father figure, and although it made me feel a little guilty at first, I knew my father would have loved Russell.

He laughs deeply, his cheeks pink, "we were out of town, but she cursed me the entire time for not bringing a case of cupcakes and chocolates for the week. So, I came straight here from the airport."

I laugh. "I'll give you a special box just for Luanne," I wink and hustle off to get a couple of boxes, one with my gourmet chocolates and another with my new chocolate cupcakes.

Russell gives a small whistle as he looks around the bakery, "decorating for valentine's day?"

I blink and look at the calendar hanging by the register. I've been so busy, but it makes more sense considering the month.

I sigh, "something like that."

Kati busies herself with the other customers while I pass Russell his boxes, waving off his card, "No, no. This is on me. Tell Luanne the new cupcakes will blow her mind, and I hope she enjoys them."

With a grin, he puts his wallet away, "I'll tell you, Betsey, every day that I come in here since your opening day, I can't help but feel so proud of how you have managed to grow this bakery."

His voice gentles, and he places a warm hand on my shoulder, "your father would have been so proud. I know I am. You're a hard-working young lady, and I can only hope my son meets someone half as good as you."

My throat goes tight with tears, and I struggle, briefly, to keep a sob from escaping as I almost convince myself I can smell my father's aftershave. My father *would* have been proud; all he ever wanted was for me to pursue my dream. I smile sadly, my heart tight in my chest, as I remember the note he left me in his will...

To my baby girl, we knew this was coming but know that if it were up to me, I would never leave your side. So obviously, to you, I leave everything. I did my best when your mother left, and, damn, I'm good because I cannot imagine a better woman than the one I raised. I am proud of the woman you have become. My only wish is that you use this money to live your dream and open your bakery. Your talent needs to be put out in the world because I don't know about you, but even in death, I Knead my sweets! (Ha, that never gets old) I wish I could be there to sing your praises but know I am cheering you on while I watch football with Jesus. Do you think they only drink craft beer up here? I'll let you know.)

I clear my throat, "I appreciate you saying that, and if your son is anything like you, I would have to consider hanging up my 'single' status." I would, too, if his son loved me even half as much as Russell loves Luanne, I would be a lucky woman.

I watch as his eyebrows furrow together, and a conspiratorial smile spreads across his face.

Uh oh. I feel the urge to backtrack, but I'm saved or doomed, depending on how I look at it, as the doorbell chimes and a load of young customers swarm the counter.

Russell turns and strides out of the store with a small smile and a wave, "say no more, Betsey. I'll have you as a daughter-in-law if it's the last thing I do!"

For the next few hours, we become inundated, and my mind goes into 'owner mode' as the day becomes a race to keep up until suddenly it's the end of the day, and we're clearing up. And, by then, the earlier moment is forgotten.

I sigh as I reach to rub my forehead, trying to stave off the headache forming. Although, as the ache becomes a dull thumb, I'm sure all I manage to do is rub a smear of flour and chocolate on my face.

I groan as I look at the clock, eleven PM, and sag against the prep island in the large kitchen. The cupcake order needed to be ready for tomorrow, so from close until now, I put the finishing touches on them. The kitchen smelled amazing, and the cupcakes looked amazing. I spent extra time making her a few extras of the new cupcakes with little birthday crowns for a more petite bouquet that I would put together in the morning.

I look over at Kati, slumped over one of the chairs. She tapped out around the hundredth cupcake, but culinary school prepped me for long hours and little sleep. So, I couldn't blame her. Between the bakery, the marketing, and the long hours I understand.

I rouse her awake, "rise and shine, cupcake. Did you want something to eat? The diner is still open."

She opens her mouth in a wide yawn and stretches. "That diner will still be open when Armageddon hits. I swear that place never closes."

It's true, though, and the diner, which is imaginatively called 'The Diner,' has been a place we have all gathered after long hours. It's our little haven.

We lock up and wind past a few people out drinking, chuckling at a group of boys in a shopping cart running down the street.

Saul, the owner, is seated on one of the hot pink vinyl chairs, his face bent over the laptop while he frowns. His face breaks into a smile when we enter. "My cupcake angels. What can I do for you? Have you eaten?" He eases himself out of the chair and into the kitchen. "Anything you want?" His voice comes from the back.

Saul is the honorary dad of anyone who comes into his diner. But for us, he makes sure we are fed, listens to all the bullshit, and sometimes sends over food when he hears the bakery has a line around the busy street. He was a godsend. No one knows exactly how old he is, as he seems to have looked like he has been in his late forties for a few years. Kati keeps saying to whoever will listen that he's a vampire. She even asked him once, and he went on a tangent about his fantastic skincare routine, but she wasn't convinced.

"We would love one of your omelets," I shout back, and we settle into our usual booth.

"Sure thing." He comes back out and pours us two glasses of iced tea. "I'll give you two each because you need to eat. You'll waste away otherwise."

"No chance of that ever happening," I love my food too much, although it doesn't show. The girls always joke that my cupcakes go straight to my boobs. On that note, I add, "and could I get some onion rings and Cajun fries?"

He rolls his eyes good-naturedly. "Sure thing. Oh, by the way, we had a new record. Your cookies sold out in under an hour this time." I smiled. A couple of months ago, after a few nights of debate, I convinced Saul to have some freshly baked items on the counter. That way, he could appeal to those on a quick break who might not want to sit down and eat a whole meal. It helped bring in more people and allowed us to come to a mutually beneficial arrangement; I'll make him the treats he needs for the Diner and the girls, and I eat and drink here for free. It works well for us.

"That's even quicker than the brownies. Do you want me to make a mix for next time?"

He nods. "Yes, please. We have a group of guys come in here quite a bit, and they all have a serious sweet tooth."

Kati perks up at that. "What do they look like? Are they hot? Young? Hell, are they older? I don't mind a silver fox."

Saul folds his arms, and his eyebrows slant over his eyes. "Do I look like I would notice what guys look like? No, you will have to come over one day and hope that the fates align and that you can meet them. I won't stop you if that's what you want to do. But just know, no one will ever be good enough for my bakery girls." He points at us with a joking smile before he shuffles back to the kitchen to start making our food.

"I might do some work here on the website rather than your shop in the next couple of days." She hums, picks up a napkin, and begins to shred it.

I laugh. "Did you know that shredding a napkin signifies sexual frustration?"

She shreds some more and then lets it fly onto the table like confetti. "Really? Well, my BOB is getting a workout lately, so maybe I should find someone to take the edge off. So how do you know about the napkin thing? Is it...true?"

I look at her and nod, hiding my lip twitch, my face solemn. "You know, I also recall that it can also mean that your body may be craving something else... or *someone* else...almost like a primal need to find a partner. Have anyone in mind?"

She frowns, "yes. No. *Ay dios*... is it true? I can do science, technology, math, code for hours, and probably hack into NASA and summon the aliens, *pero sobre el amor, ¿hombres? No sé nada.*"

I shrug and pick up my napkin before unfolding it and refolding it into a fan. "You know about love and men; you're just as jaded as the rest of us. Relationships can be hard, but when someone tries to show you who they *really* are...let them... you never know. Also, I have no idea about either of those two things. It's one of those floating articles or posts I may have read, but I'm not sure if it's true or in my head."

She rolls her and laughs. "You get 700 roses, and suddenly,

you want to give love a chance. Save that shit for daytime television, *mi loca querida*. This is why I love you, though."

Saul comes over with four perfect omelets, piping hot fries, and onion rings, slides into the seat next to me, and we spend the next hour catching up on the gossip from the past few days, leaving out the stuff about Petty Betty.

By the time we got to my car, having had to weave around the drunken revelers from the only club in the historic downtown area and ignoring the drunken catcalls, it felt like a lifetime had passed. But realistically, it was less than five minutes.

Fifteen minutes later, we drive through Lakewood and past the stunning homes until we pull up and park outside my childhood home. Like always, I take a few minutes to appreciate my day before I get out of the car. Kati is snoring softly to my right, so I take a few extra moments than usual. Russell's words from early flow through my head, and I can almost see my father on the upstairs balcony, where he would sit nursing a whiskey in the warm Texas air, waiting for me to get home every day. My father was my best friend, especially after mom left. Although, even before that, we were inseparable. He had lost his parents young, and he made it his mission to give me as much love as possible to make up for not having grandparents. I was his little girl, in a muddy ballerina outfit and football helmet every weekend. I smiled at the thought; even when it wasn't football season, he would take me out to the backyard, and I would pirouette while we threw a ball back and forth. On other days, we would spend the day in the kitchen, covered in flour, while we tried to recreate his mother's old recipes. We were a perfect pair.

When it was time to choose a university, it was a no-brainer, and although he encouraged me to apply to schools in other states, I went to the University of Dallas. Even though I spent plenty of days and nights on campus with the girls, I lived at home, and we spent as much time here as we did on campus. I feel a lightness in my chest and a slight tingle of energy as I take in the view. The house is a beautiful two-story colonial, with large white columns flanking the front entrance. My father was an outdoorsman, dedicating much time to the upkeep of the property. Although I have to hire help, just like when he was alive, the lawn is perfectly manicured, with a garden of vibrant flowers in full bloom. The driveway was made of smooth gray cobblestones, and at the end of it stood a large fountain, with water cascading down a tiered fountain into a stone basin that I put after he passed as a memorial.

After he passed, the house felt too large for me alone, and I asked Kati to take one of the four bedrooms upstairs while I moved into my father's old room. Although I know to some, it may be hard to grieve when in the space of their loved one that has passed, for me, it helped me grieve.

I shake Kati awake and trudge up the driveway and into the house. While my feet ache with each step, I feel a sense of peace as I walk into my childhood home, which still smells faintly of my father's aftershave. This house may be significant in size, but it is full of love, warmth, and comfort, and every corner of it holds an echo of all the memories we had made, the laughter we shared, and the love we had for each other.

Eyes drooping, we kick off our shoes and make our way upstairs. After a quick shower, I feel a wave of gratitude wash over me as I slip into my pajamas and crawl into the plush bed. I remember to set my alarm to wake me up in three hours, trusting the staff to start prepping by four because despite how much I loved my bakery, I needed a little more than two hours of sleep. Luckily, we only opened for a few hours on Saturday, mainly for deliveries, and closed Sunday. In truth, I could probably sleep for a week.

As my head hits the pillow, I let out a contented sigh and close my eyes. My last thought is that I'm grateful that I have a delivery team because, like Kati said, I looked at Nathan's card every day. I also kept every single card from the many bouquets he sent. *Nathan Weild*. Just his name sent a wave of heat from the top of my head to the tips of my toes.

I may be a coward, but the fear of handing myself over on a platter was terrifying; After dad passed, independence was all I knew. Still, even a week and eight hundred roses later, no matter what I say to dissuade myself, I feel the weight of his gaze like a caress on my overly sensitive skin. This electricity still tingles throughout my body, and I can't help but think that...maybe... just maybe Nathan will be worth overcoming the fear, of falling in love.

Chapter Eleven
...WHAT DOES YOUR SOUL SAY...

Betsey

"Turn that fucking noise off," Kati's voice breaks through the loveliest dream ever. I was on a deserted island with unlimited food and drink at my disposal, with Nathan and his friends as my cabana boys. It was perfect until a shrill voice ruined it.

"Ugh, fuck you, asshole," I mumble, cracking open a gritty eye. The lack of sleep punches me in the gut, but at least the extra hour helped. Sure, it wouldn't stave off the raccoon eyes I'm sure I was sporting, but, like always, a little makeup would take care of it. Concealers, not diamonds, are a girl's best friend.

"Fuck me? You've snoozed that shit so many times that I was dreaming of bells." She climbs into bed with me, grabs a pillow, and shoves it over her head. "Turn it the fuck off. It's the weekend."

Her words register, and I frown. I don't remember snoozing the alarm. A shot of panic shoots through me, and I launch myself out of bed, grabbing my phone. I nearly choke on my tongue as I look at the time.

"Shit! Kati, it's nine am. I still have to build the bouquets and hand them to our delivery team. Fuck they are supposed to be at their house by eleven. Damnit."

I take the world's quickest shower and play an excellent game of 'try not to die' while soaping up, avoiding getting my hair wet, and brushing my teeth. Only to slip on the floor as I run out of the bathroom and smack my elbow painfully on the ensuite door. Still wet, I curse as I fall over while I try to shove my legs into some jeans and then shove my tits into the first top I blindly grab from my closet. *Did my fucking clothes shrink?*

"Kati! Get up and help me!"

She grumbles, but kicks into high gear, running out of the room. Bless her.

I hop around and shove my feet into the pair of heeled booties. Not ideal, but they are the first thing I see, and I don't have the time to give two fucking shits.

Kati, fully dressed, comes in holding my uniform, and I shrug on the chef's top, ignore the buttons in favor of shoving my phone in my pocket, then grab my bag and run out of the door. I almost twist my ankle going down the stairs, and I limp the rest of the way to my car, Kati locking the front door.

I try to catch my breath and thank the gods that it is Saturday, making the usual fifteen-minute drive into ten as I speed around the streets.

"*Coño,*" Kati cries, holding the 'oh shit' handle, and I turn sharply, narrowly avoid a curb and pull into my parking spot at the bakery.

By 9:20, we are walking into the kitchen.

"I am so sorry, guys," I yell as the staff bustles around.

"Don't sweat it, boss lady, but you did miss Carlos. He had a delivery at 9:30 and couldn't wait any longer. Unfortunately, since we know you prefer to build the bouquets yourself, we had no choice," Leanne, one of my pastry helpers, says, and I curse my luck.

I nod as I run to the table to get the bouquets built.

Bouquets are essentially large, tiered platforms shaped like a pyramid, only upside down. I artfully arrange the tiers starting with the one cupcake on the bottom and working my way up; I add the leaf-shaped fondant, which is almost as decadent as our chocolates, that we make in-house. The platforms were built to withstand the atypical design, resulting in two huge, gorgeous bouquets and a smaller one with our new cupcakes.

Kati whistles, "you outdid yourself with this, *mi amor....*" She smirks, "I've never seen you add a special bouquet on top of an order. You sure you didn't go all out just for your new mother-in-law?"

I scowl, and she giggles.

"It's her birthday. Everyone deserves something a little special on their birthday," I say, my chin held up as I avoid looking at her.

The bouquets did look beautiful; the way I set up the flavors with little edible cards that had the initials on them to indicate flavors weaved into the fondant leaves was genius. But, as I looked at the heavy-laden table, I frowned. *How the fuck was I going to get these there?*

Carlos is my delivery man for a reason, he looks like he could bench-press a truck, and honestly, I'm sure he can. But with Carlos gone, I will have to have the team help me into one of the vans and transport these myself. We had the setup to keep them from falling over, but only in those vans. Then there is the massive issue of getting them out. Although I'm sure, Nathan and his friends could get them into the house if I ask. Assuming they were there already.

I sigh and look at the time, 10:40. The house is fifteen minutes away. Fuck me.

Betsey

A whole team and an almost disastrous fall later, I pull in front of the address at 11:05.

Holy, cream-flavored jizz, I think to myself as I fully absorb what I just drove up to. My house is massive, but this place, in the heart of Highland Park, is just...insane.

The mansion is a grand, Victorian-style home nestled between rows of substantial leafy trees, giving it the air of privacy. It has a stately appearance, with a sharply peaked roof, ornate white trim, and an elegant wrap-around porch complete with rocking chairs. The yard is perfectly manicured, with lush green lawns, colorful gardens filled with blooming flowers, and a white picket fence that encloses the property.

I feel Petty and Betty on my shoulders, and they whistle as they follow my gaze.

Petty- Who the fuck needs that much damn space? Do you think they have wild hot orgy parties in there? I mean, it's big enough. If they do, can we go?

Betty- First off, ew. No one wants to go to a party hosted by older naked people. Second, in terms of the house, it's not about needing it, but if you can, why not?

Petty- Well, maintaining that shit is why the fuck not...although I guess if they can afford this AND two of our girls' gourmet bouquets, they probably have a shit ton of staff in there.

Betty- Precisely. Also, it is now 11:10...I think it's time for you to go inside. Make a good impression! You may be able to rub some elbows and get referrals.

Petty- Psh, we don't need referrals. We are booked solid. No, what you need to do is make a good impression on mommy-dearest so that you can hop on her son's dick. Preferably while he licks frosting off our huge tits...

I shrug them off and jump out of the van.

Only ten minutes late, I could work with that.

I knock on the door and rock back and forth. Moments later, an older woman with red, rosy cheeks, a bright smile, and brown hair peppered with white smiles at me as the door opens and I'm greeted by the warmest pair of chocolate eyes I have ever seen. My heart burst with the desire to envelop her in my arms. She is that adorable.

"Oh, dear! Hello! You must be the surprise my boys have been telling me about. I told them I didn't want a stripper for my 50th, but they didn't listen, it seems. Well, I guess you can set up the pool of Jell-o in the backyard," she sighs dramatically.

Oh, this lady is right up my alley.

I nod solemnly, "well, I'm sorry to disappoint, but we ran out of Jell-o, so we must use chocolate pudding. We were also fresh out of candies nipple tassels, so we must use the pasties."

After a beat, she laughs so hard that tears start to stream out of her eyes, "oh...you are a gem." she gets out between wheezes.

The door opens wider, and I hear the warm boom of a familiar voice, "whoever is making my wife laugh this hard better not be a potential suitor. I would hate to have to hide a body for her birthday, but I will make the sacrifice."

"Russell?" I smile widely.

"Betsey? I knew the surprises were being delivered, but I didn't think it would be by the boss lady herself!" He steps around his wife to give me a warm hug before stepping back to wrap his arms around his wife's shoulders.

"I didn't know it was for Luanne! I am so glad to meet you finally. Russell talks about you non-stop," I forego, extending my hand to hug her instead, feeling like I already know her.

She hugs me back hard, "Betsey as in *the* Betsey...does that mean?" her head swivels around me, and she looks out to the driveway, where the van is parked.

"Cupcakes!" She screams at the top of her lungs, runs to the van, opens it up, and claps exuberantly.

Russell wraps his arms around my shoulders and leans down

to whisper in my ear, "you see what I mean? She is a Kneads Sweet's cupcake addict."

I whisper back, "I would say, get her into rehab, but I don't think I have ever seen anyone so happy to see my cupcakes... well, maybe except...."

"Cupcakes!" Lawrence comes bounding out the front of the house, where he meets Luanne, and they hug and jump up and down together. They start a chorus of 'best birthday ever,' and I giggle.

"Well, except maybe Lawrence," I laugh, and Russell shakes his head.

"Yeah, that boy loves his cupcakes. Sometimes I wonder if I took the wrong baby home from the hospital," he jokes. It suddenly registers. Luanne, Nathan's mom. Russell's son.

A slight shiver works its way down my spine, and I am suddenly hyper-aware of my body. Not even a second later, a smooth, deep voice, paired with the scent of a delicious cologne, envelops my senses. "They found the cupcakes, bunch of fiends...."

"Ah, Nathan! This is Betsey. She is the owner of the Kneads Sweets Bakery," Russell slaps Nathan's shoulder with a noticeable tilt of his head, eyes wide.

"We've met. She took the order personally," he responds with a small laugh, and they exchange a look, seeming to have an entire conversation in silence.

Russell throws his head back, letting out a triumphant laugh, his face looking ten years younger, "Oh, Ho! The roses all over the bakery? Took a page right out of my book there, son?"

"I learned from the best, but it looks like I'm going to have to bring out the heavy artillery," he frowns with a slight shake of his head.

Russell claps his hands, and his eyes gleam with excitement as he turns to me, "I did vow that I would have you as a daughter-in-law, didn't I? The Weild men are never wrong regarding love, my dear. So I am glad to say that based on the Weild Family Benediction, you are officially part of the family."

Nathan raises his eyebrows, and his gaze meets mine. I watch as his expression morphs from one of amusement to one full of hunger and lust. "There was never any doubt. But, once I convince her to go on a Weild date, she will see that too," his voice calm, sure.

All air whooshes out of my lungs, and I feel my face heat.

Petty- Oh man, I would like to point out, by my devil horns and gorgeous spiky tail, that hell is sweltering. Even so, I feel myself sweating. This man is almost preternaturally skillful with his words. Do you think he's some wizard?

She jumps off my shoulder onto Nathan's and sniffs him before shaking her head and coming back to mine. It's hard enough to keep my composure; I didn't need my inner Id and Ego in the mix too.

Petty- maybe not a wizard, but there is something there.

Betty sighs and lays on my shoulder, on her stomach, holding up her head with her hands, a wistful expression on her face as she flutters her wings. *That is one dreamy man—all the jerks you've had to deal with. There is one thing to send you flowers, but to claim you in front of his family? Fuck that ex, don't fight it.*

*Petty- Did you curse? Oh man, if Betty keeps agreeing with me, then you know Nathan is the right thing to do...*she rubs her chin...*or person to do. Either way, get him, girl!*

"Well then, looks like you have a hot date to plan, son. Even so, now we can move on to the proposal. It will have to rival mine, which is a tall order. Also, I am going to want at least two grandchildren," Russell looks seriously at Nathan, who rubs his chin and nods. I choke on my spit and start to cough, my head pinging back and forth as they discuss my love life. Or rather, my entire life.

Nathan pats my back gently and looks at his father, "understood. We should skip the semantics; we can set up a wedding here?"

"What's this I hear about two grandchildren? I want at least four." Luanne says, her voice muffled as she speaks around a mouth full of cupcakes. Lawrence's face is covered in frosting as he comes closer.

"Man, these are better than ever. Where the hell is Ivor and Oskar, they need to help get these cupcakes in the house. Also, I vote for four nieces and nephews," he adds as he runs back into the house, yelling for his friends.

I finally catch my breath and open my mouth to respond, but Luanne cuts me off, grabs my arm, and starts to steer me inside, "Leave Betsey alone, you animals. If she chokes to death, who will make my cupcakes?" The men laugh, and they turn to go to the van, but not before Nathan wraps one arm around my waist and pulls me in close, "you never called me, Ms. Knead, but now that you're here, don't think I'm going to let you go... ever," slowly and seductively, his eyes roam over my body. I involuntary gasp as the familiar, delicious shiver works its way up my body.

"That's enough, you scoundrel. Go get my cupcakes, and I will disown you if you drop even one!" Luanne says, voice stern. Nathan pulls away with a wink.

I'm still trying to catch my breath when Luanne grabs my hand and pulls me behind her.

She looks back at my face and gives a small chuckle. "You have that same dazed look on your face that I wore when Russell first hit me with his Weild charm. His mother told me it was the same when she met her Weild man. God bless her soul. Honestly, Honey, you don't stand a chance; these Weild men are some charmers. Ruthless when they know what they want. It's also part of their supposed Weild benediction."

She shook her head and led me through a large door that led into what must be their backyard but looked like a small park with a giant pool. If this was the backyard, I'm sorry I missed the entrance of their house while under a Nathan-induced haze.

"Oh, Betsey dear, let me take that chef's shirt from you. I'll grab you a drink." I shrug off my shirt, and Luanne takes it, putting it behind the bar.

She does a double take and whistles, "oh, honey. That chef's shirt does an excellent job of hiding that figure. Do you always dress like that for work? Or was today a special occasion?" Her eyes sparkle with mirth as she mixes something behind the bar and pours it into a vast cup. So much that it is bound to knock me on my ass. *Yass, Luanne. I was here for it.*

I look down and sigh, "this morning, I slept past my alarm for the first time in years. I grabbed what I could and pretty much hoped for the best. Figures I would grab a fuck me shirt and my date jeans. I thought my clothes were shrinking." I shake my head. Luanne passes me the giant cup, the size of Nathan's friend Ivor's forearm, and I moan in pleasure as I take a few chugs. *So good.* I close my eyes as the alcohol hits my system like a freight train. *Holy shit, what kind of concoction was this?* A few more sips and I decide I don't care as I sip heavily —*straws for the win*.

Luanne smiles as she drinks from her cup. "Well, even if you were trying to avoid the Benediction, you would have no hope in that outfit. Makes me miss my days, but..." she laughs and pats her slight belly, "my time of business meetings are done. I want to enjoy my family, cupcakes, and chocolates."

I tilt my head, "what exactly is the Weild Benediction?"

Luanne sits next to me, waving at some of the guests arriving with a bright smile before turning back to me. "Well, for generations, the Weild men have been able to know whom they will spend their life with the moment they meet them. Russell's father, Kenneth, said that the moment he met Janet, he felt something like electricity shoot through his body.

Russell, till this day, swears he felt an electric current jump-start his heart when he saw me," she chuckles, her cheeks warming, a fond expression in her eyes.

Luanne lowers her voice, being mysterious, "Kenneth says his father and grandfather were similar. Going back generations. Legend has it that the Weild family helped an old witch when she needed to run from persecution. They hid her in the basement and kept her safe for weeks. Making sure she was comfortable and fed. Before she left, she vowed that the Weild family would be bestowed the love they so generously showed her in her time of need."

I can't help but lean forward as she talks, her words resonating with a truth I felt down to my bones. But, still, I must ask, "what about when the women meet them? What about you? Did you feel anything?"

I lower my voice, at least I think I do, "I felt like I was jerking off an electric eel."

She spits out her drink, and I pat her back.

After a moment, she gives me a knowing smile, "Electric eel? I'll counter your eel and raise you, feeling like I dropped a toaster in my panties! Goodness, I felt a current go straight from my heart to my vagina," she fans herself with a tinkling laugh and takes a deep drink.

I almost choke on my drink as I burst out laughing, tears at the corner of my eyes. Luanne was me, 20 years from now.

"I'm serious," she giggles. "I fought it for a bit, there was always some girl chasing after him, but he was relentless, and all it took was one date, what they call the Weild date. If I hadn't already melting been every time he looked my way, this date would have sealed the deal. It was like the stars aligned," she gives a slight shiver, and despite the warm air, I see goosebumps on her arms.

I didn't know if the witch story was true but the conviction in her voice left me breathless. Whether it's from excitement or trepidation, I can't say, but I know with certainty that this Benediction is real for Luanne. And if it is real for her and all the generations before, what did that mean for me?

Petty- Bitch, it means...you cannot fight fate. Or a witch's spell. I knew I smelled something on him. It must have been a whiff of mystical residue.

Betty rolls her eyes- I don't think you can smell any magic.

Petty- I can do whatever I want. I am a manifestation of Betsey's mind. Which means she clearly feels something fishy going on with how hot she is for Nathan.

Betty- Whatever. Although I have to say, our girl has never felt this way for anyone, and certainly not this fast. If that's not magic, I'm not sure what is.

Petty- mmm, magic dick sounds yummy.

I feel a little lightheaded, a pleasant warmth flowing through my body that was part alcohol, part fascination at this family legend. All we needed was a campfire.

I bite my lip, "wasn't it...scary? Giving yourself to someone like that? Especially so quickly? I've been on my own since my dad passed, and I've built my business from the ground up. But before that, the only true love I ever really had was my father. Every other guy has been a dud; my friends and I pretty much gave up."

"Hmm...Falling in love is always slightly terrifying. I mean, come to think of it, it was a bit scary for me too and downright creepy as hell when Russell told me that I was the one like it was a done deal," she giggles and snorts.

"But," her eyes met mine, strong, clear. "I listened to my soul. Others will say to listen to your heart, but the heart can be fickle."

Her face was strong, shining with a steadfast and serene peace. "So, my dear, what does your *soul* say? If you follow that, then it won't lead you astray. Your father showed you how to love and *be loved* fiercely; you already know what love is. You know what it feels like to have someone dedicate themselves to your joy. When you have that knowledge, no one can take it away or corrupt it. You can only add to it."

She stands up and wobbles, and I stand to help but almost end up on my ass.

She cackles, "Oh dear, it looks like we are properly sloshed. You know what that means?"

Our eyes meet, and we both shout, "cupcakes!"

Chapter Twelve
...PENIS LICKING AND FROSTING FROLICKING...

Nathan

"Your mom can drop some real gems there," Lawrence whistles low. We all stand by the large kitchen window that opens to the bar. We could hear them perfectly even as we stood to the side to avoid getting caught.

Ivor grunts in agreement. His eyes widen as he soaks in my mom's knowledge.

"My Luanne is one with words, but she means every one. Man, I love that woman," my dad whispers, taking a sip of his drink. "And I'll tell you one thing, your Betsey didn't stand a chance once your mom made her the Weild cocktail. Those two will be gabbing gals for the rest of the day."

My heart warms at my father's use of 'your Betsey.'

Oskar laughs, "oh man, do you remember when your mom and grandma drank the Weild cocktails on her last birthday? I swear, I will never unhear their sex stories."

"Do I remember? We had to stop them from streaking. They spilled every secret they ever had. When grandma gets here, we will probably find out every dark secret Betsey has," I chuckle lightly.

"Man, today is going to be epic; I feel it. You think Betsey would want to invite her friends?" Lawrence says hopefully, his mouth full of cupcakes.

"Not a chance, buster," Betsey slurs slightly from the kitchen door, and she marches up to the cupcake bouquet, my mom on her heels. Putting their drinking down, they quickly stuff a cupcake in their mouth with tiny squeals of happiness.

I stand transfixed. I've never seen Betsey outside of her chef's shirt, but...*Fuck*. I resist the urge to adjust my dick in my jeans. She has a ridiculously tight, low-cut black top, sheer in the middle, pushing her mouthwatering tits up high. Pair that with tight jeans and her boots. She looks like a rockstar's wet dream. *I want to smear frosting on her tits and lick it up.*

Everyone turns to look at me, and I hear a boisterous laugh from the door.

"Looks like we came just in time," my grandfather walks in and wraps my mother up in a hug.

"Happy birthday, my sweet girl; I hope my son is treating you well."

"HeboughtmecupcakesIlovehim," my mother gets out, mouth filled with a raspberry cupcake massacre, and he laughs.

"Did you say cupcakes? Is it from that bakery you love? Gimmie," my grandmother comes around and grabs a cupcake before turning over to us.

"Hello everyone, first...cupcakes," she takes a joyful bite.

"Jesus, what is in those cupcakes? The only thing she puts in her mouth that fast...."

"Okay, Dad!" My father cuts him off, and we laugh.

"Ooh, penis licking and frosting frolicking. My kind of kitchen talk. You know my friends, and I hate penises," Betsey frowns, swaying slightly.

"No, that's not right, they don't like us...no, that's not right either. They just suck!" She fists pumps into the air.

She jumps on the counter and grabs her drink in one hand,

"You know, before Nathan, only my dad ever bought me flowers. Now I hear I'm his Benedict Arnold, and I get to go on a super dick, big guns date where he convinces me never to run away, but I don't think I want to run away, so no date needed, we can cut straight to the sex part. I feel at home here; you guys are awesome," she takes a deep sip and gulps audibly before lowering her voice into a whisper. Or attempting to anyway, "Also, I don't want to fight a witch. It's always a good versus evil thing, and I am much more the bake them an apple pie and watch them die type of chick. You know what I mean?"

The boys and I lean against the counter and soak in the view, Betsey fitting right into the madness that is my family.

My grandfather nudges me, "So is this your Weild-er woman, grandson?"

"Oh yeah, she is," Lawrence chuckles, "your grandson has been sending her hundreds of roses every day this week, from the day he first met her. The Bakery is full of them."

"That is the Weild way. Anything less, and I would have to disown him. We Weild men treat our women like the gifts they are," my grandfather says gruffly.

My father nods, "Interestingly enough, I went to see her yesterday. We talked all the time when I picked up your mother's daily cupcakes; I always had a good feeling about her. I've seen that young lady grow from the first day she opened that bakery—hard worker, that one. In the bakery from four AM until way past closing time," my dad shakes his head with a proud smile.

"In any case, I was telling her that I would love to have a daughter-in-law just like her. I even vowed to have the two of you meet. It turns out the great ol' Weild Benediction was working from the day she opened that bakery."

"Wait. Bakery? As in the Kneads Sweets Bakery? Oh, don't tell Janet that. She will make me drive up every weekend to learn your girls' secrets," My grandfather laughs.

"What are you all talking about over there?" My grandmother yells, a drink in her weathered hand. My mother was going to have them completely sloshed.

"Nothing," we chorus.

Betsey scoffs, "Men love to lie. It's why we, the girls and I, get them back."

"What do you mean?" Ivor asks.

"Well, first offly,ly,ly. You speak? Amazing party trick! Can you fill up balloons, too? I want a princess crown!"

Ivor chuckles, and we look at him in surprise.

He shrugs, "what? I like your woman, Nathan. She's funny."

Shit, I guess he does do party tricks.

"Secondly,ly,ly. My friends and me. We created a revenge service. One guy even went viral two days ago. He shat his pants and ended up on TV," she lets off a squeal of laughter.

"The 'fecal fury' asshole? That was you guys? Oh man, I knew I recognized that voice in the Wreck-It Ralph Mask. That was Lia, right? Man, that guy was all over every social media platform and even the news," Oskar laughed and shook his head.

"Masterfully done, my girl. I saw it on the news; he had a double life, and men like that put the good men to shame. It's why Weild men will always be the best," my mom puts her drink up in the air, sloshing over the rim.

"Great in bed too. Puts my new hips to shame!" my grandmother chortles.

We shake our heads; it will only get worse from this point. Soon my mother will give everyone the Weild drinks, and the entire party will turn into a gaggle of depraved women spilling their souls. Of course, we love them, but parties are...interesting here.

"Hey! What about us?" Lawrence protests.

"Oh, you boys have spent enough time around us; I'm sure some of our magic has rubbed off on you. Honorary family and all that," my mom waves her hand. "Tell me, have you recently felt any...instant attraction and lovey dovey feelings? Your father's childhood friends ended up tied down shortly after him. So don't be surprised if the love benny gets you guys, too," she cackles, taking another drink.

The boys look at each other, and I hide my smile. Cupid butt fucked them days ago, and I was looking forward to seeing them tumble through their coming falls. Ivor, especially.

"Oh yeah! Weild men seem amazing," Betsey nods enthusiastically, and my father and grandfather puff up their chests. *Cocky bastards, I know where I get it from.* "BUT! I didn't think so at first," she adds.

I feel my eyes brows shoot up of their own accord, "Wait, what? What did I do?"

She blushes, dropping her head to her chest before straightening her chin. She looks back towards my mom and grandma, leaning in close.

"Well, momma and gammy Weild, let me start by saying Nathan seems pretty damn awesome. Major props there, by the way. BUT our first revenge was actually *against* Nathan. Some lady paid Petty Betty; that's our revenge name, by the way. Started in college. Crazy stuff happens on college campuses, let me tell you. So *Anywhoooooooooo*, some lady paid Petty Betty ten thousand dollars to get immediate revenge against her boyfriend, who apparently stopped talking to her. We didn't even know who it was... we filled his car with red glitter, even stuffed it in the vents," she guffaws while the boys and I stared at her open-mouthed.

"You guys were the porn suit glitter bandits?" Lawrence says incredulously.

Betsey rolls her eyes and scoffs, "Listen, don't get me started on the outfits. We were short on time, and Lia's assistant is absolutely useless; he went to a BDSM store for those outfits. Between you and me, that guy is a totally useless pervert. I mean, cartoon masks and cut-up crotchless sex suits? Those things are not one size fits all; I mean, my boobs barely fit," she waved her hands and grabbed her boobs. My mouth went dry, and I didn't realize I moved until I feel my dad put a hand on my shoulder to pull me back. He shakes his head with a chuckle and I frown, *fucking cock block*.

"So yeah, forget my boobs. It's time for the best part because then...we peeled out of the gym parking lot as the boys came running out," she chortled.

"The sweetest victory was the looks on their faces, which we got a picture of by the way, as Lia screamed, 'you've been Petty Bettied bitch; Kati threw in 'The Fast and the Furious, *Pendejo!'* Maeve told them all payback was a bitch, and then... and then... oh man, I yelled Cupcake Bandits Forever! It was amazing," she struggled to catch her breath while she laughed.

My mom and grandma were leaning against the counter, holding their stomachs, barely able to catch their breath. Likewise, my father and grandfather try and fail, to hide their chuckles while I struggle to pick my jaw off the ground. *Traitors*.

I barely held back a growl, "I knew I recognized those voices. You glittered me." I stride up to the counter, where Betsey wraps her legs around me and hugs me to her chest. Suddenly I wasn't that upset. This was a delightful place to be. Then I remembered... Weild cocktails make these women ridiculously strong.

She rocked me back and forth, squeezing me tighter and tighter and suddenly, it wasn't such a delightful place to be. All the baking has made this woman freakishly and deceptively strong.

"Aww, don't be mad, my little green-eyed, hazelnut-whipped vanilla cupcake. We carried out the revenge, but we didn't know it was my witchy future Weild man. I won't say sorry, however. You looked absolutely adorable in red glitter and gym sweat.

Like a sexy, body-building stripper," she gave a final squeeze, grabbed my face, pushed it back, and then pulled me in close, smashing my cheeks. "I'll make it up to you. We can go out on that welding date. I always thought welding looked like fun. Also, I promise I will get back at this woman and defend your honor...unless you did ghost her, then I'm telling your mom and grandma. I know them, you know; we go way back. To like an hour ago. It's been a beautiful friendship full of laughter, cupcakes, and crazy strong alcohol." She places a kiss on my forehead and pushes me back...hard.

"Good God, man, I thought she would suffocate you. Come back to the safe zone. You know better than to approach a woman on the Weild cocktail," my grandfather grabs me, pulling me to the side of the island where the women weren't.

"Even so, that was stronger than normal. Did you know she was that strong? She can probably bench press with me at the gym. I'm going to invite her," Ivor says, voice proud.

"Dude, she kneads dough all day. She probably picks up bags of flour. She may look dainty, but she is not," Oskar adds.

"You think her huge boobs are actually muscles?" Lawrence asks with a murmur, which is promptly followed by all five of us smacking him in the head.

"Ouch, it was just an observation," he grumbles.

"Cupcake bandit," my mother wheezes out.

"Fecal fury, absolute gold. But let's go back so that I understand," her eyes gleam. "You make these cupcakes?" My grandmother asks. My grandfather groans and she silences him with a look.

"Yes, ma'am, I do! Russell comes in every day to get Luanne her daily fix. It's how we met; he's the closest thing I have to a father, you know," she says, voice firm. My father lets out a slight sound, and his face reddens. If it weren't for the Weild cocktail effect, he would have wrapped her up and hugged her until she begged for mercy.

Her word vomit continues, "Since mine passed away, that is. Russell talks to me, encourages me. He's a good father. I wish mine were still here," she wipes a tear. "You guys would have got along great, I know it. Anyyywhoooo, so I guess that Bennie thing works long-term. First, Russell met me; then even Lawrence started coming in every day...Then Nathan comes in the day after we glitter-fy him. Crazy how life works," she shakes her head. "Wow, the room is spinning really, really fast."

"It's your first time, dear," my mom's head bobs in understanding. "To get you used to it faster, I gave you a double...."

"You what?" I say, my eyes bulging.

"Woman, are you trying to kill her *before* we get grandchildren?" My father shouts.

My mom puts her hands on her hips, "in theory, it was a good idea, but I was two drinks in...howeverrrrr, considering how small you are," she looks back at Betsey, who is swaying, eyes half-lidded, holding both her hands in front of her eyes with an awed expression. "Hmm, maybe it wasn't a good idea," my mom adds.

I rush forward as Betsey tips forward, and I catch her, holding her close.

She looks up at me, eyes half closed, a small smile tilting the corner of her lips. "I tried super, duper hard to resist you; the flowers were an amazing, nice touch, by the way...but there is something about you, Nathan, wathan. You are a special cupcake recipe from the Love Gods. I know it; I can feel it in my treat-making soul," she whispered, her voice lowering.

"I want this. I want your family. I want a dad and a mom again. I want a grandma and grandpa. I even want your weird friends and Ivor. He's cool. But...I want you, too." Her eyes closed, and her breathing deepened.

My heart skips a beat as I process her words, and a flood of emotions washes over me: surprise, happiness, and adoration mixed in with a healthy dose of smugness. I chuckle deeply as I look down at her serene expression. The Weild cocktail was no joke; I'm surprised she lasted even this long if my mom gave her a double.

Speaking of, I look up to see my mother smiling with my father and grandparents. Their love was so palpable that it was downright mesmerizing.

I sigh and decide not to call my mom out on possibly giving alcohol poisoning to my future wife and, instead, will let her slide until she is sober. Tomorrow though...

"You son of a bitch," Oskar claps my shoulder. "You do always get what you want."

"I get what I work for," I grunt.

"Technically, the Weild magical whatever did the work. The roses don't count. Hell, even your dad put in more work over the past few years," Oskar laughs when I scowl at him. *Fucker, roses totally count.*

"Why do I have to be the weird one? Ivor even got a special mention. I'm the one that buys her cakes," Lawrence pouts, reaching for another cupcake.

"I am badass. Like recognizes like," Ivor grins.

"Son, go lay my new daughter down in your old bedroom. She is going to be out until tomorrow with your mother, borderline giving her alcohol poisoning," he glowers at my mom, who has the decency to look chagrined. "Betsey needs the sleep; at least from that room, she won't hear the party. Once your mothers' friends get here, it's going to get...well...you know," he shakes his head with a laugh. Yeah, I imagine my mother and her friends were remarkably similar to... the cupcake bandits...

I laugh as I carry her up the stairs, into my bedroom, and lay her down. I tug off her boots for now. Afterward, I would have my mom and grandmother come and put her in pajamas. Hopefully, before they get any drunker...

Chapter Thirteen
...YOU DESERVE SOME DICK WITH YOUR CUPCAKES...

Betsey

I groan as I groggily open my eyes, my mouth dry. "Argh," I shut my eyes again, the sun blinding me.

I reach over to my nightstand and grab a glass of water, sipping gratefully.

I try to open my eyes again and pause as I take in the room. I am in a four-poster bed that sits directly in front of large windows, and from here, I can see a large balcony and hints of a garden. I was essentially in a fairy tale. I rub the back of my neck as I look around the room, half expecting woodland creatures to pop in and start singing and letting me know where the fuck I am. Instead, my eyes fall on a picture of a smiling younger Nathan in a cap and gown, and my memories come flooding back.

I grimace as I remember the laughter and the strong as fuck Weild cocktail. I haven't been put on my ass by alcohol in years. *What the fuck is that drink made of.*

Petty- Who gives a fuck? You have no hangover. Whatever that drink is, it is, first and foremost, and miracle.

Betty nods - I thought I would wake up with vomit on my wings. This is way better.

I sigh, "I pretty much confessed everything."

Petty scoffed- Yeah, you fucking did. But they loved it, and they loved you.

Betty- Honestly, it looks like you fit right into the family. They are just like you. Luanne and Gammy Janet are you when you're older; it is...strangely unsettling and comforting, but I dig it.

Petty- Ha! Nothing unsettling about it. It will only get better from here. They accept us.

Betty- Technically, they accept her.

Petty- We ARE her... did you forget?

Betty- Oh, yeah.

I brush them off with a small smile. They were right, or I was right. Either way, before I passed out, I did have a lot of fun yesterday. I feel like I have known them for years. Sure, I could have done without my drunken profession of how Nathan made me feel or my vow to get revenge. But I would have confessed to Petty Betty, so yesterday sped everything up.

I push the covers off me and frown at the pajamas I have on. I purse my lips and laugh lightly. I vaguely remember Luanne and Janet coming into the room as giggling messes to help me change.

Luanne knocks over something from the dresser and turns around wildly. "Shhh, you'll wake her."

"I don't think the Knick knacks can hear you," *Janet sniggers.*

"Oh. Well, let's change her," *Luanne places the pajamas in her hands and starts to tug off my jeans. As tight as my clothes were, they quickly stripped me and put me in pajamas.*

"My, our Nathan sure is lucky. She is beautiful," *Janet whisper yells.*

"Funny, sweet, and hard working. Russell absolutely adores her, and I can certainly see why. I'm a little in love with her myself," *She giggles and then sighs softly.* "Maybe together, they will finally make time for something other than work."

"Oh, that won't be an issue. The Weild men always make time for their families. We were all workaholics at one point before we found each other," Janet adds.

Russell pops his head in the room, "If you two are done, I suggest you come downstairs before Lawrence finishes these cupcakes. That boy is a bottomless pit."

Luanne gasps, "Not my motherfucking cupcakes." She charges out of the room, Janet hot on her heels. For an older woman, she sure was spritely.

I notice a pair of leggings and a t-shirt on the bed and make my way to the ensuite to shower and change, a skip in my step.

Nathan

I stare at the clock on the living room wall for the hundredth time that afternoon. Betsey had been sleeping all day, and it was now almost four. I sit on the couch, pouting as my dad and grandfather bring in snacks, setting up to watch international soccer. They are obsessed with all sports, especially now that they have more time to indulge.

"Son, she will be up soon. That girl needs to rest," my father gives me a playful shove as he sits down.

My grandfather chuckles, "ah, you remember how it was when you first met Luanne," they exchange a knowing look.

My mom and grandmother come in the room, "he was downright obsessed with being near me. Boosted my confidence something serious," she laughs and sits on my father's lap.

I frowned slightly; I wanted Betsey on my lap.

He nuzzles her neck, "you didn't need a confidence boost. You were always perfect." My mom squeals, and I look over to my grandfather, who is busy hugging my grandmother.

I lean back with a groan and turn my head to stare out the

windows. I can't remember when my mind was laser-focused on anything other than work. Although, to be fair, there was no reason to step away from the routine that I had perfected: work, work, and more work. Even though I was stupid enough to ignore the validity of the Weild benediction, my willingness to avoid going into the office even on a Sunday was proof enough.

I felt my heart beat wildly as a familiar voice filtered into the room, "Good morning, or afternoon, I guess."

I turn, and my jaw drops as I shake my head in disbelief. She looks fucking delicious wearing my high school football jersey. The room disappears and I am suddenly in front of her. In one motion, I have her in my arms, and her soft and subtle curves mold to my body. *Perfect fit.*

I cup her chin and search her eyes for any ounce of hesitation. Instead, I find the tell-tale glow of joy and passion I often see reflected in my mother's eyes when she looks at my father. Her tongue darts out to lick her lips, and I crush her to me with a soft groan and press my mouth to hers. My head spins, the stars align, and I know with certainty...she was made for me.

Betsey

As our lips touch, the presence of his family in the room becomes insignificant. The world fades away and my body melts into him as I cherish each stroke of his tongue against my own, the gentle caress of his lips moving over mine.

I realize that up until this moment, I have never been properly kissed. Yet, this is what a kiss is supposed to be; anything else paled in comparison.

The way his mouth moves over mine is akin to a drug, demanding yet gentle at the same time. Nathan's arms pull me impossibly closer, and I feel an almost feverish longing and desire as if this moment was building up for much longer than it has. Suddenly, I understood how true the Weild benediction must be because this... this kiss? Defies logic and reasoning.

Breathless, we pull apart. My legs feel like Jell-O, and I am grateful for his firm hold as I attempt to throttle the dizzying current that races through my body. My body tingles, and oxygen floods back as I meet his gaze, and I'm hit with another wave of longing, a fervent yearning that downright consumes me, as his eyes glint with wonder, tenderness, and passion I know mirror my own.

Reluctantly, I pull away slightly and touch my lips in amazement, "wow."

"Wow is right; I think I'm pregnant," I hear Lia's voice from somewhere in the room.

My eyebrows fly up, and I move to step away from Nathan to see if my ears are deceiving me, but he quickly pulls me back with a growl.

Petty- Holy hotness, don't you dare step away from this hunk. If that was just a kiss, can you imagine when you finally run your tongue along those abs, you know he is sporting before he fucks you senseless?

Betty- I feel like I can't breathe. How long do we have to wait until he kisses you again?

Petty- Based on his hard dick against her lower back, not long. Goodness, did you feel his arms? Like stone, so big and hard.

Betty sighed wistfully- *and the hard planes of his body...but he still held her like she was the most essential thing in the world. Can you imagine him with a baby in his arms?*

Petty- Yes. I can. Betsey? Make some babies.

My back now to his front, his arms firmly around my waist. I cannot hide my smile as I melt against his hard body. Not that I would want to. Everything just felt...right.

I meet Lia's and Kati's amused smiles as they hold up a phone, Maeve on the other side of the screen.

"Girl, we thought Nathan kidnapped you and locked you up in a dungeon full of roses until you finally gave it up like a filthy whore," Lia snorts.

"I can see we weren't far off; only instead of a love cave dungeon, you are just making out like this is one of the telenovellas *mami* and *abuela* watch on Sundays," Kati smirks.

"I walked away from the shoot when my assistant ran up to show me a 911 text. I told them that if you were ever kidnapped, you would fashion a rolling pin out of whatever was nearby and beat the ever-living shit out of someone...although the timing was perfect, the asshole doing the shoot with me was getting handsy. I was about to give him a prostate exam with a piece of coral," Maeve growled in frustration.

"What? We will go to Maui next. I mean, now that we know that Betsey is perfectly fine and getting pregnant in a mansion with a kiss. You could have texted us, asshole," Lia scowls.

"Sorry, that was our fault; we got her sloshed with the secret Weild family cocktail recipe. She never stood a chance," Luanne says, moving closer to us all.

"That and my grandson has completely wiped her brain with all his Weild magic and now again with that kiss," Janet ambles up with a knowing smile.

"Luanne, you remember the first Weild kiss you ever had? It was like falling into an ocean and flying simultaneously," she sighs wistfully.

"Do I ever. I almost gave it up right then and there," Luanne says.

The girls blink and start to laugh.

"Oh man, it's like looking at three generations of Betsey," Lia chortles.

"*Ay dios mio, que familia tan sabrosa!*" Kati adds.

"Thank you, my dear, we are quite delicious!" Luanne smiles, and Kati claps with glee.

"Do you have another son? I like the vibes here." Kati asks.

"No, but she has us," Lawrence adds from somewhere in the room.

I can't move to see from where, as Nathan chooses that moment to run his nose up my neck and place kisses on my collarbone. I shiver in response, and he chuckles into my neck. *Oh, gods. Take me.*

"Gladly," he whispers in my ear. Oops, I said that out loud.

I feel everyone's amused stare.

Luanne pats me on the shoulder, her eyes bright with understanding, "it's okay dear, everyone here, well maybe except for your friends, but they will catch up, is used to Russell and I and Janet with Kenneth. We are a very affectionate and passionate family."

"Excuse me, can we get back to the handsy asshole? You said you were in Maui. Where? I'll catch a plane right now and rip his neck from his shoulders," Ivor growls coming around to snatch the phone from Lia's hand.

Nathan's head snaps up, and his mouth goes slack, "holy shit, it's coming true."

Maeve sniffs, "never you mind, I don't need protection I just need to find a sharper piece of coral. Anyways, now that I know Betsey is safe, I will go back to the shoot. You go, girl! You deserve some dick with your cupcakes," she adds with a laugh before the screen goes blank.

Ivor's face darkens, and my heart pangs with sympathy.

"Hey Ivor, how about we go into the kitchen and bake some cupcakes? I will give the girls the run down. Then, if they agree, we will tell you where Maeve is in Maui," I say softly. His face brightens slightly, and he nods, walking to the kitchen. I vaguely remember where it was. As it was, I was fortunate that the living room was right off the massive grand staircase. Otherwise, I would have gotten lost in this big house.

"We will?" Lia whispers, and Kati nods in confusion, fastidiously ignoring Lawrence's stare.

"Trust me, girls, when you hear what we have to say, you'll be hard-pressed to say no," Janet grabs their hands and pulls them behind her.

Chapter Fourteen
...HOLY, CHEF PORN...

Betsey

It takes a moment for Nathan to let me go, and he sighs as he grabs my hand and pulls me behind him. Russell and Nathan chuckle softly, their faces soft, and I see memories flash through their eyes. My heart warms: this family truly was blessed with love and magic. There was no other way to really explain it.

I turn away, wanting to admire the house as I follow. Before I was pulled into Nathan's orbit, the living room had blown me away. It was spacious and inviting, with comfortable couches and chairs arranged around a large bay window that overlooked the garden. The room had been filled with natural light and, despite the size, had a welcoming, lived-in feeling, with books and magazines piled on the coffee table and a scattering of family heirlooms on the mantelpiece.

Just being here, I couldn't help but feel the warmth and love emanating throughout the house. As we pass the foyer, the feeling is fortified as I am immediately struck by the home's cozy atmosphere. The floors are made of dark, polished hardwood, and the walls are adorned with paintings and family photographs. The grand staircase that I came down this morning leads to the second floor, where there was a fireplace in the corner of the room, and I had a feeling that if I walked through the other rooms, they would all be decorated as warmly as the rest of the house.

"Russell, your home is gorgeous. It feels like every warm and fuzzy feeling when I walk into my own home," I say in awe.

He chuckles, "Thank you, my Luanne decorated herself. She did a fantastic job turning this abandoned amusement park into a home. But you haven't even seen the cherry on top yet; you were a little too...enthusiastic... to notice yesterday." Before I can ask what he means by "cherry on top," my eyes nearly pop out of my head as Nathan leads me into a kitchen straight out of my wildest, deepest, darkest, kitchen porn fantasy.

"Holy, chef porn." I snatch my hand from Nathan's and dart into the culinary haven of my dreams. My home kitchen was beautiful, but I couldn't bring myself to renovate it as it held so many memories. The bakery's kitchen was state-of-the-art, but this one could easily accommodate two of Knead Sweets' kitchens.

In the center of the room is a super-sized marble island, waterfall style, with a built-in six-burner stove complete with a full griddle, double oven, and commercial-style range hood. But, holy *fuck, it also has a built-in chef's sink,* and if that isn't enough, the other side has so much space for food preparation and storage space underneath.

Petty and Betty pop onto my shoulder, mouths wide.

Petty- Is that a separate prep area WITH a farmhouse sink?

Betty- MORE counter space?

Petty *flies off my shoulder and to the cabinets*- Dude, look at this lighting. She pops out and back. There are even fucking lights inside here!

Betty *points to the pendant lights over the island*- and more up there!

Petty *keeps jumping from space to space*-What the fuck is going on here. Is that a pantry or a secret bat cave?

Betty- definitely a secret cave...these people aren't just rich. Betsey hit the motherlode of marble kitchens and custom cabinetry.

I feel my head ping back and forth through the kitchen as I ignore the chuckles and stares behind me.

"I can put an airbed on this thing and sleep next to my creations," I mutter. I run around the island and squeal as I come face to face with The Meneghini La Cambusa Fridge. Not just any fucking fridge, it was easily one of the most expensive in the world, handcrafted by Italian artisans. I'm talking about the cost of a car, expensive.

I moan as I open the doors and almost climb inside and move in.

"A freezer, ice maker, wine cooler, coffee maker, microwave, another fucking oven, pantry, and fucking steam oven," my eyes roll back, and I roll my hips provocatively.

I force myself away from my future kitchen baby daddy and almost die as I skip over to a counter with two high-powered blenders and two colossal kitchen aids. I feel like my mind is whirling, and I feel like singing, so I grab a stainless-steel spatula and belt out my version of '7 Rings' by Ariana Grande. The better version...Obviously.

> *Fuck breakfast at Tiffany's,' I'd rather bake crumbles.*
> *I am a chef who likes getting in trouble.*
> *Petty and betty, some mixing machines.*
> *Buy myself all of my favorite chef things.*
> *Been through some bad shifts; I should be a sad bitch.*
> *Who would've thought all my cakes would be ravaged?*
> *Rather be tied up by Nate and some ring.*
> *I write my own checks like I write recipessss.*
> *My whisk, keep beatin', My cake, keep eatin',*
> *Yo' eyes like soc-kets, my sweets so poppn'!*

You like my squares? Gee, thanks, they're walnut.
I see it; I cook it
I want it; I bake it
Want Cookies? I'll make it.
Need sponges? Just cake it.
Food Gasms? Don't fake it.
A cravin'? Just sate it.

Nathan

We stare transfixed as Betsey runs around the kitchen, her face downright feral with joy. When she moans and starts humping the air, my dick gets hard, and I have to grit my teeth to avoid throwing her down to finish that kiss...the right way.

"Is she singing seven rings?" Lawrence asks in awe.

"No. It's her special rendition, 'Kitchen Bling.' You should have seen her the day the builders unveiled the bakery kitchen. She jumped onto the island and started twerking to her version of Savage by Megan the Stallion and Beyonce. How did that go?" Kati looks at Lia.

Lia rolls her eyes, "'Queen B, you want to cook with me? Now turn that fucking oven up to three hundred degrees.'"

Kati bursts out laughing, "that's right! Then broke into a split and added, 'Knead's a savage, cooking skills nasty. I talk big shit, but my cakes be slammn'.'" They said the part together and broke out in giggles.

"Dude, you wasted your time sending flowers, you should have just sent her a fridge and toaster; you would have been married days ago," Lawrence muttered.

"If you had sent her sub-zero, she would already be pregnant," Lia chortles.

Fuck.

"She's going to be busy for a while, this is only her first song, and this kitchen can easily fit two of the bakery kitchens. So in the meantime, what is this information you need to share?" Kati asks, skirting around to stand next to my mom and grandma, further away from Lawrence, who keeps trying to get closer.

"Boys, you can go back to the living room. Let us girls have some Weild time," My mom takes the girls into the backyard, but instead of going to the living room, we lean against a wall and stare at Betsey transfixed.

We watch as she grabs another spatula, runs into the walk-in double pantry, and belts out her rendition of WAP by Megan The Stallion.

I said, certified chef
seven days a week,
wet moist cake
make that diet game weak.

They all guffaw like a bunch of hyenas, but all I can focus on is that she has a fuck ton of energy. *Energy I plan to put to good use.*

Chapter Fifteen
...IT JUST HAS TO LAST FOREVER...

Betsey

Two hours, several songs, and one plane ticket later, Ivor was off to Maui, and Lia and Kati hightailed it out of the Weild mansion, presumably to hide at Lia's place, Lawrence and Oskar on their heels. I couldn't help but hope that they would also find their intense mind-bending, happily ever after because, in just a little over two days, the Weild benediction was unraveling in total, and I knew that Nathan was the one for me.

Me? After goodbyes and promises to come back next week to bake (like I had to promise anything with that gorgeous kitchen), I was sitting in the passenger side of Nathan's, deglittered Maserati, since Russell vowed to have the van delivered tomorrow.

Currently, I am sitting, mentally biting my nails as we drive towards my house, and the entire time the car continues to fill with tension, the air around us electrified, making my senses spin. Every time his gaze meets mine, my heart turns over in response.

I swear I feel the very movement of his breathing, every inhale and exhale almost tangible. The silence in the car is almost like foreplay, and as Nathan picks up my hand to rub small circles on the inside of my wrist, I bite back a moan as my oversensitive skin sends a flush of warmth that spreads from my core to my every extremity. I feel my back arch slightly, my body involuntarily leaning towards his pure magnetism. His very caress is a command and a promise to my body of what is to come, and I feel my core grow wet in silent supplication.

Nathan

I feel my body temperature rise, the prolonged anticipation almost unbearable. My mother warned me that we would be drawn together until we were nearly delirious, but this was beyond anything I could have prepared for. With every passing moment, I feel my tenuous control crumbling. She doesn't even realize as her body leans toward me, almost instinctively, that her closeness is like a drug to my senses, and I have to force myself to concentrate on the road.

Unable to stop myself from at least feeling the warmth of her skin, I grab her hand and rub small circles on the inside of her wrist. Immediately, I almost regret my lack of control and curse internally as her body arches, her lips parting in a silent moan.

It never occurred to me that something as simple as a car ride could be a form of foreplay, but *this* was downright a sensual experience. I grit my teeth as we pull into her driveway, forcing myself to regain a semblance of control. Benediction or not, her first time with me will be exactly what she deserves.

Betsey

I look out and start to recognize the houses we pass, and I

almost breathe a sigh of relief as my gaze flicks to his profile from the corner of my eye. I see his jaw clench and his gaze become hyper-focused as we approach the house.

Petty-he is probably mentally fucking the shit out of you.

Betty- he does seem the type of man to be very thorough and... comprehensive with his approach.

Petty-yeah, yeah. He's mapping you the fuck out and just counting down the moments until he can unwrap you like a present. He's going down...wait...no...it's going down, but if you're lucky, there will be a lot of going-downs and, hopefully, really, good ups.

Betty-multiple ups. If that kiss was a preview...you are really going to love the movie.

Petty cackles- *what the winged one said. Have fun! You're home.*

They wink as they disappear.

"Wait there," Nathan pins me with a stare, his voice thick and almost imperceptibly unsteady. As he gets out of the car and walks around to me, I feel an intense satisfaction, knowing that he is as affected as I am. That someone as disciplined as Nathan is barely holding onto his control.

My heart pounds as I unbuckle my seat belt, as he opens my door. Then, before I can think, he pulls me roughly, almost violently, to him and presses me against the car. My breath whooshes out of my lungs with a low groan as my body meets his.

His eyes glow with an almost savage fire. I whimper as he leans down, his husky voice full of promise as he whispers in my ear, "I thought I would go crazy in that car. It took every bit of my control to keep from pulling over and losing myself in you until every memory of any other man between your legs was gone," he runs his hands down my body and presses one hand against me before pushing his hand inside my leggings and sliding his fingers through my soaked slit.

I gasp as his fingers circle my swollen center. My instinctive response to him is so powerful that his touch does precisely what he promises, and I feel like it is my first time. No one else before him mattered; they never existed.

"Fuck," he groans and closes his eyes briefly. He pulls his hands out of my leggings, and I almost weep with the loss. He cups my chin and holds it gently, bringing my gaze to his. His eyes, dark with lust, search mine, and I feel my body clench, the tender touch of his hand at odds with the emotion swirling in his eyes.

"I feel like I've waited forever for you. I may be barely holding on to my control, but your first time with me, in any capacity, will not be outside against my car. I want to look into your eyes while I touch you. While I ring every ounce of pleasure from your body. While I make you mine."

He leans down, and his mouth hungrily covers my own, his kiss urgent and exploratory. I wrap my hands around his waist, pulling him closer, and feel his hardness against my belly. Then, with a groan, he tangles his hands in my hair, and I raise on my tiptoes and meet his passion with my own.

Almost painfully, we pull apart, and he sweeps me into his arms, kicks the car door shut, and strides confidently to the front door. Keeping his eyes on mine, he pulls out the keys— keys I don't even remember him taking— and opens the door. He pushes it close and looks at me with a silent question.

I struggle to speak as I answer, "upstairs, the first room to the right."

The moment we get into the room, his lips recapture mine, more demanding this time. I lose awareness as our hands feverishly pull off each other's clothes. Despite the vibrating tension in our bodies, Nathan gently pushes me onto the bed and presses the hard planes of his body against mine.

Then his lips slowly descend to mine in a sweet kiss of promise.

The implication sends waves of excitement through me as he starts a gentle exploration, his mouth grazing my earlobe. "You're so fucking perfect; I can't wait to taste you, claim you, with more than just the benediction. I'm going to show you why we belong together until you beg me to stop. We will spend the rest of our lives exploring one another, but right now, this is my promise to you; you'll never need anything, and I will love you the way only a Weild man knows how...with all of me."

Between each word, he plants kisses on my jaw, the hollow of my neck, and my shoulders. I can't formulate a response as my body arches as his mouth closes over one of my nipples, his other hand gently outlining the other. He alternates, his tongue caressing my sensitive nipples.

"Oh fuck," I breathe out as his tongue makes a path down my ribs to my stomach before he nudges my legs apart with his massive shoulders and places an open-mouth kiss on my swollen center.

My head falls back, and I lose my mind as he works me over like a fucking starved man.

Nathan

As I move down her body, I can't help but try to memorize every dip and curve of her delicious body. I groan at the first taste of her, and I take my time savoring her soft flesh, and draw her swollen clit into my mouth and tease her, ever so gently, with my tongue. I hold her hips firmly in place as I watch for every slight movement and shudder of her body.

Within moments, her hands weave into my hair, pulling me closer.

Her throaty moans send more blood to my impossibly hard

dick, and I almost come when her eyes roll back, and she screams my name, flooding my tongue with her sweetness.

I continue to savor her until she is wreathing, and I draw my lips back up her body, retracing my path. Then, like a man starved, I worship her breasts, tugging gently with my teeth while her head tosses back and forth.

"Please, I'm clean on birth control, and I need you inside of me, Nathan."

I chuckle as I place a kiss on the pulsing hollow at the base of the throat, "I'm clean, too."

With that, I place one smooth leg on my shoulder and push inside her wet, tight pussy.

Betsey

I gasp in sweet agony as he stretches me to my limits. His eyes search mine, and he must find the answer he is looking for as he pulls out just enough to thrust deeply. I shout as wave after wave of ecstasy throbs through my body as he expertly uses every push and pull of his hips to drive me into a frenzy.

"So fucking tight, so sweet. You feel this?" Nathan draws out slowly, and my body tries to draw him back in.

He hisses, "mmm, fuck yes. Your body was made for me; this sweet pussy is all mine."

His dirty words almost send me over the edge, but when his hand finds my clit as he thrusts deeply, my entire body detonates.

His agonized groan pushes me to my limits, and my nails run down his chest.

"Yes, Nathan. Fuck, yesss," I writhe beneath him, my release still coursing through me as he continues to work my body to new heights that I didn't even know were possible.

I find myself wanting, no... needing more; his domination, his complete control over my pleasure.

My eyes meet his in a silent challenge, and he raises an eyebrow in response, never pausing his deep, smooth strokes. I shudder.

"Does my sweet baker need a little rough play?" He growls out, his gaze going impossibly darker as his own need flares.

"Use me, Nathan. Fuck. Me," I ground out.

Nathan

I growl at her request, pull out, and flip her onto her knees, her ample ass and soaked slit on display for me. Unable to resist, I pull her cheeks apart gently and circle my tongue around her tight rim.

"One day, I'm going to fuck you here while I fuck your pussy with a toy. You'll be so full that you'll come for me until you can't move. Would you like that?" I push my tongue inside of her, and she moans.

"I said would you like that?" I give her ass a hard smack, and she whimpers and pushes back on my tongue.

"I expect an answer when I ask you something, Betsey. Do you want me to use you? To fuck your sweet pussy until you beg for me? To fill you up with my cum? You're going to have to follow directions," I punctuate my words with a slap, and she wreathes beneath me.

"Yes, Nathan."

I push her down until her chest is on the bed and her ass is impossibly higher. *Fuck.* I lick my lips.

"Good girl. Now don't move. I need to taste you; you look so fucking sweet like this," giving her ass one last lick full of promise; I dip my tongue inside her before drawing her clit into my mouth. She moans, and I wrap my lips around her, sucking gently while worshipping her swollen clit with my tongue. I feel her legs tremble and flick my tongue faster, but I pull back as I feel her shake.

"Uh, uh. You don't get to cum yet," I say softly, and I pause, running my hands over her back and ass. I lean to run my tongue up and down her pussy one last time, then I line myself up with her swollen pussy and slam inside her with a groan.

She screams, and I work my hips drawing out her pleasure. Unable to hold back, I reach down, pull her body against mine, grab her hair by the roots, and bring her closer. She groans, and my jaw clenches as her body bares down on me. "I'm going to fuck you hard, and you're going to cum for me, do you understand?"

"Yes," she breathes out, and I fuck her unmercifully, driving into her body as she screams in pleasure. I soar higher until I hurtle back to earth, moaning as her body drains me.

The reality of the moment hits me as I pull out, and her body melts against me, her breathing deepening. I tug a sheet over our bodies and pull her into my arms, her head on my chest. She murmurs unintelligently as she snuggles closer to my body.

I can't help but marvel as I look down at her sweet perfection, her soft curves flush against me. My mind wanders as I think of the way she had responded to my touch, the way she had moaned my name, and I can't help but feel like the luckiest man in the world. I knew for sure that I would never get enough of her. I want to hold her in my arms every night, just like this, and wake up every morning to her still here. I want to spend every day learning something new about her. I want to spend the rest of my life making her feel loved and desired.

As I lay with her, my heart clenches, and I lose track of time as I gaze down and memorize her features. Even though I feel my body being dragged into sleep, I fight to stay awake just to savor the moment a little bit longer, letting myself drown in this new, unfamiliar, but welcome feeling of love.

I understand the premise of the Weild benediction-- Hell, I see my parents and grandparents always act like besotted fools —But I ignored it for the most part because, in the back of my mind, I knew I would eventually find my own blessing.

And as Betsey's breath tickles my chest, I can't believe I have ever spent one moment without her. Yes, it was soon. Yes, it was fast. But no one ever said love has to take forever; it just has to last forever.

Chapter Sixteen

...VERY STRONG INDEED...

EPILOGUE

Betsey

"You mean, he didn't even have to bring out the big guns?" Richard's four-year-old eyes widen, mouth slack. His green eyes were so much like Nathan's' it made my heart burst with love every time I looked at him.

I giggle at his expression as I hold Summer to my chest for her feeding.

Richard has progressed from bedtime stories to bedtime *and* naptime stories, and he always asks for the same one...how his dad and I fell in love.

"I reckon he's got that story memorized by now," Russell's gruff voice comes from the bedroom door, and Richard glowers at him.

"Yup. But daddy said the Weild men have responsibilities... so I have to learn..." his face is solemn as he nods.

I hide a smile as he trips over 'responsibilities', and it sounds more like 'resthbolobilitiess.'

"Your dad is right. So what's the first step?" Russell asks, approaching Richard's bed and sitting on the edge.

He holds his little hands up and starts to tick off his fingers, "The first rule is to love mommy with all my heart; I gots to protect her when daddy isn't home. Second rule is to love baby Summer because we have to show...ummm... show her what love is!" his eyes brighten it all comes together for him.

"That is right. You also must always be a good man who works hard but always...." Russell trails off with a smile.

"Makes time for his family," they finish together, and my heart bursts.

This was the usual daily routine, both nap time and bedtime. Of course, Russell and Luanne were always there for both, and it was something I would always cherish.

The day I gave birth to Richard, Russell stood over his bassinet and promised to be two grandfathers combined to make up for my dad's passing.

The Weild men were a blessing, but the family I have gained over the years made it even more special.

"Mommy, when are my aunties coming over again? Are they bringing..."

"They will be here after your nap, and everyone is coming... It's your grandma's 55th birthday, and your 4th birthday was last week. So, it's going to be a big party. But only if you nap," I say sternly, and he sighs, lying down in his bed.

"Okay, shoo, shoo. I gots to sleep so I can wakes up! Bye!" He burrows under the cover, and with a slight chuckle, I stand, Summer still firmly attached as she suckles furiously.

"I'll stay here and hold his hand until he falls asleep, you go ahead," Russell whispers, and I smile and walk out of the room.

Russell and Luanne got just what they wanted, a grandchild in a hurry. Within three months, Nathan and I had gotten married on a destination cruise with all our friends and family, and about a week after the wedding, we found out we were pregnant with Richard. Baby fever drove Nathan to the brink of madness after Richard turned one, and he wore me down until we decided to try for baby Summer. I knew I loved him the moment we met, but seeing him as a father? Well, that just made me love him even more. Nathan wanted to be around our children *almost* as much as he wanted me naked. Almost.

I slowly make my way down the grand staircase and head into the kitchen to watch from the window as Luanne mixes a batch of the Weild cocktail. As Summer was just two months old, I was grateful that I could back out of it this year, as every time I did indulge, we had a repeat of the first time I ever met the Weild family. In short, a hot mess.

Luanne and Russell had set up a nursery for Richard and then Summer when they were born, making it a lot easier for them to watch the kids when I was at the bakery and Nathan was at work. However, they did have to fight Nathan for them as he always wanted them at the office with him. I would pump, and he would pop over to get the fresh milk. I felt like a human smoothie shop, but I couldn't argue with that man. He always found a way to turn it into an hour-long sex session in my office or his.

So naturally, I tried to argue as much as I could.

Speaking of the devil, I feel his presence moments before his arms wrap around me, "mmm, Mrs. Weild. We must stop these kitchen romps. What will the kids think?"

"Ew, no thanks. I don't like it when mom and dad talk about fornication next to the cupcakes," Lawrence walks in, nose scrunched. He immediately grabs a cupcake from the kitchen island before making his way to me.

"How's my perfect niece doing?" he stares adoringly at Summer, dropping a crumb on her face.

I brush it off with an exasperated smile, "how many times do I have to tell you to stop eating over the children?"

"Stop making all the sweets and having cute children. I can't decide whether to hug them or eat the treats, so I do both," he shrugs, and I roll my eyes.

Nathan kisses the hollow of my neck and places a hand on Summer's head, "how long has she been nursing?"

I sigh, "about an hour now. You know how the growth spurt weeks are. Can you burp her before I switch her to the other side? It's starting to hurt."

I put my finger into her mouth gently to pop the seal of her mouth over my nipple and pass her to Nathan before tucking myself away.

"You know, I see more tits now than I ever did in college, and its only because they are always being milked," Oskar comes into the room and grumbles.

"Well, we are family men now. It's unavoidable," Lawrence grumbles, angrily stuffing another muffin in his mouth.

"Sexually frustrated there, brother?" Nathan chuckles, gently burping Summer.

"You're only gloating because your wife is past the six weeks for healing. My wife is only three weeks in. She went upstairs, by the way...changing the baby," Lawrence sighs.

"Why didn't you go change the baby?" I ask with a knowing smile.

"You know damn well; she plans four separate outfits a day. I have no idea which one goes at which time. If I mess up, I can't perv while I help her pump one side while she feeds the baby from the other. I need something to hold me over," he whines.

"Whatever, at least you get to touch one boob. The twins just drink all day long. They are worse than college guys on frat row," Oskar tosses himself into a chair pitifully.

"You guys are making it hard for me to be excited about the baby. I can hear you guys complaining from outside," Ivor strides in, his large body filling the room with its presence. Having all four of them in a room was like a mental and vaginal mind fuck. *Too many hot men in one room, and in Texas, that was a dangerous thing.*

"The only hot man you need to worry about is me," Nathan leans down to whisper in my ear, his voice husky and purposefully seductive.

A shiver works its way down my spine, but before I can respond, Summer makes a mewing noise, and my shirt gets soaked as my breasts respond to her small demand.

Nathan sighs with a small smile, "Thwarted by a hungry little one, once again. I'll get my revenge when you're older, my sweet girl," he says with a sweet coo that does more for me than the deep timbre of his familiar voice.

"There is something about a man with a baby that sets me on fire," I snap my head up with a smile as Maeve walks into the kitchen, heavily pregnant.

"I'm glad...now sit." Ivor grumbles, pulling a chair seemingly from thin air.

"When the fuck did law school teach you magic tricks?" Lawrence says, eyes bugging out.

"Probably around the same time, all those advanced calculus classes were teaching you how to add squares and triangles, *cabron*." Kati comes into the room with a scowl. "You leave my brother alone. He is only caring for his wife."

"Why does everyone love Ivor more?" Lawrence asks, tossing his hands into the air before grabbing Kati and the baby and pulling them into his arms. We lose them as they fall into their bubble, much like we all do when wrapped up with our men.

"It's the rugged, 'I will destroy your entire family' mafia vibe. Totally makes him all snuggly and lovable," Lia walks into the room, suspiciously baby free.

"Where are the boys?" Oskar asks.

"Where there is a grandma, there is a way. Janet and Luanne stole them from me. Stopped making the cocktails and everything. I needed a break. My boobs are sore," she rubs her breasts, and Oskar's eyes laser focus on them.

Russell stands at the kitchen doorway with a bright smile on his face, "the Weild Family Benediction is still going strong, I see."

I look at Nathan as Summer latches on to my other side, "very strong."

Nathan leans down and moves his mouth over mine with a sweet, lingering kiss, and I savor every second, a warm glow going from the top of my head to the tips of my toes.

Very strong, indeed.

Petty In Paradise

Get ready to fall in love with love all over again in 'Petty in Paradise,' the sizzling sequel to 'Petty Betty'!

Maeve is totally over, asshole guys. Especially when they only want to date her because she's a model. Eff that.

So when one of her co-workers gets handsy at a photo shoot, she is ready to rip his head off until Ivor shows up and offers to do it for her.

Maeve knows she doesn't need a man to make her happy, but she can't deny that from the moment she meets Ivor, she feels her heart jumpstart. She wanted him more than she ever wanted anyone else.

Ivor didn't pursue women, they chased him, and he would make it known that it was a one-time thing. He wasn't interested in love when he had work. But when he meets Maeve, all of that goes out of the window. He has to have her, and he will ensure she knows she isn't getting away.

So, pack your bags, grab your sunscreen, and don't forget your sense of humor, as you join authors Ruby Smoke and USA Bestselling Author Isabella Phoenix for a tropical romp where the steamy romance is the only thing hotter than the Maui sun– this is one romantic comedy you won't want to miss!

LET'S HAVE A TOAST

Ruby

First and foremost, a big thank you to all my fantastic alpha and beta readers, ya'll are the real MVPS and will forever have a special place in a dark, comedic heart. (Shannon, Bre, Dawn, Brianna, Jessica, Jade)

Deadass, though, shout out to the KeyBoard Whores. We may bang our keyboards harder than a horny jackrabbit bangs his next-door rabbit mistress, but we get the fucking job done.

Mads and **Jo**, you put all the beef in my taco, and I love y'all long time for it. You guys are the guac to my taco. (Bitch I know the GUAC IS EXTRA! & so are we)

Anne & Piwa, my love for you both is something that transcends. Thank you both for being the very definition of a soul sister and soul brother. Anne, soul-mates forever, through every pitfall of our mental health struggles, we prevail and love each other. *(Even though Piwa and Julian have taken over)*

Husband/Soulmate- You are a particular sort of man. The kind of man who loves the person who can come up with these ideas of revenge and still sleep peacefully at night...you shouldn't...but you do... and I love you for it. You're the fixings to my hero sandwich, the hot to my stuff, the stuffing in my turkey, the juice in my caboose...wait...okay, I just love you...don't run.

Also, **thanks kids** for going to your dad instead of me when I'm deep in my cave.

Readers- I love you dearly, take notes, and then let's compare them. Together, we can get revenge on all those hoes!

ABOUT RUBY

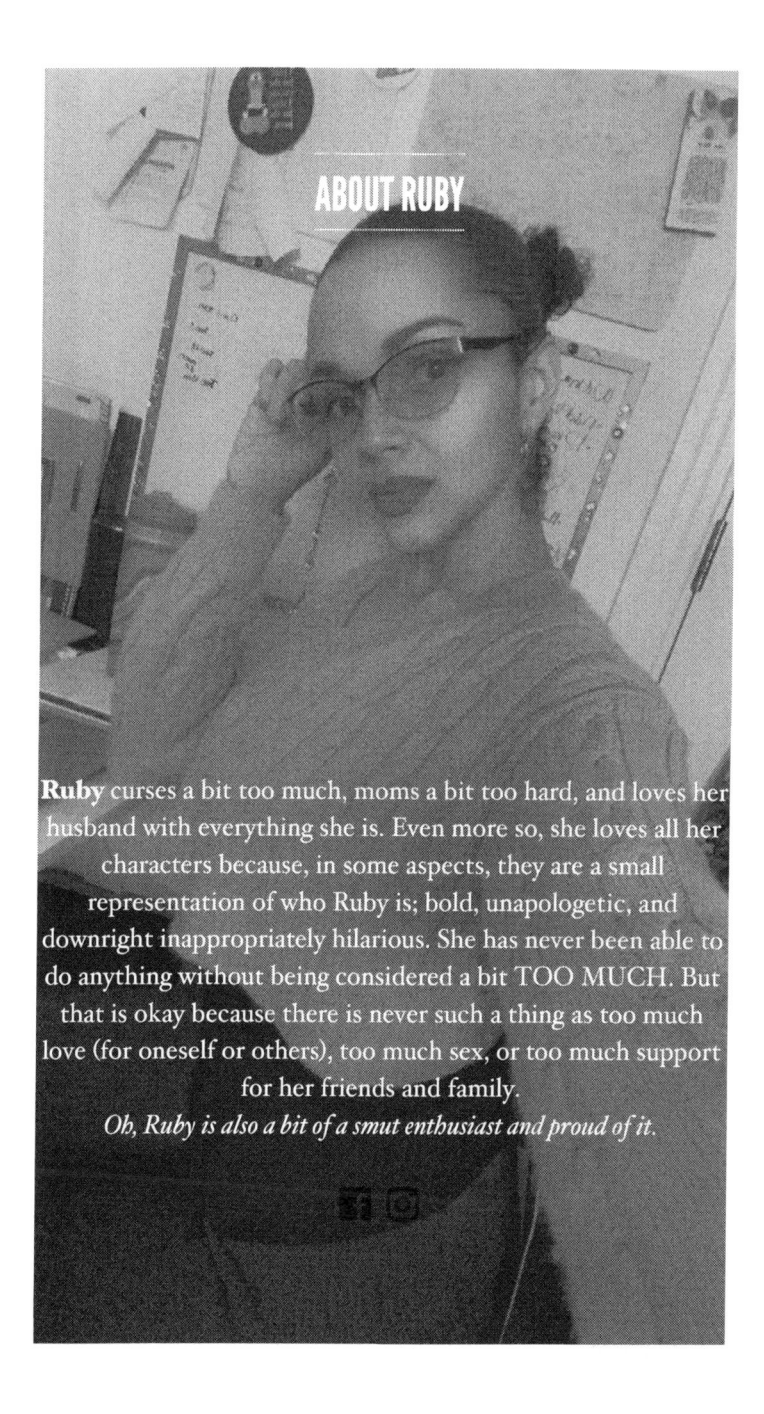

Ruby curses a bit too much, moms a bit too hard, and loves her husband with everything she is. Even more so, she loves all her characters because, in some aspects, they are a small representation of who Ruby is; bold, unapologetic, and downright inappropriately hilarious. She has never been able to do anything without being considered a bit TOO MUCH. But that is okay because there is never such a thing as too much love (for oneself or others), too much sex, or too much support for her friends and family.

Oh, Ruby is also a bit of a smut enthusiast and proud of it.

ALSO BY RUBY

BOOK'S READY FOR YOU!

Veiled (Concealed in Myths Why Choose Romance)

Femme Fatale (Erotic Collection F/F Menage Monster Romance)

Infiltrated (Concealed in Shadows Book 1 Why Choose Romance)

Ours to Keep (Anthology)

She's Knot That Into You (Cabria Shifter Falls Omegaverse 1)

JOIN MY FACEBOOK GROUP AND SIGN UP TO MY NEWSLETTER

Ruby's Nut House: A Ruby Smoke Reader Group

COMING SOON

Within the Veil (Concealed in Myths 2 Why Choose Romance)

Insurrection (Concealed in Shadows 2 Why Choose Romance)

The Art Of Roleplay (Erotic Encounters Why Choose Romance *EROTICA*)

She's Knot That Into You (Cabria Falls 1 Omegaverse) (Aneira and Casimir)

Love at First Neigh (Cabria Falls 2 Horse Shifter Novel) *(Storm &*

Calian)

Petty in Paradise (Petty Betty Book 2) *(Maeve and Ivor)*

Cat Got Your Tong's? (Cabria Falls 3 Cougar Shifter Novel) (*Ralph & Hazel)*

Petty Much In Love (Petty Betty 3) *(Lia and Oskar)*

'Un Poquito' Petty (Petty Betty Book 4) *(Kati & Lawrence)*

Printed in Great Britain
by Amazon